THE CASTAWAY BILLIONAIRE

by

SERENITY WOODS

Copyright © 2021 Serenity Woods
All rights reserved.
ISBN: 9798473600414

DEDICATION

To Tony & Chris, my Kiwi boys.

CONTENTS

Chapter One 1
Chapter Two 9
Chapter Three 16
Chapter Four 24
Chapter Five 31
Chapter Six 39
Chapter Seven 46
Chapter Eight 53
Chapter Nine 61
Chapter Ten 68
Chapter Eleven 75
Chapter Twelve 87
Chapter Thirteen 95
Chapter Fourteen 104
Chapter Fifteen 111
Chapter Sixteen 118
Chapter Seventeen 125
Chapter Eighteen 132
Chapter Nineteen 139
Chapter Twenty 147
Chapter Twenty-One 154
Chapter Twenty-Two 161
Chapter Twenty-Three 168
Newsletter 177
About the Author 178

Chapter One

Victoria

"So let me get this straight," Lucy says. "When you were twenty-one, you dated the guy in the aisle seat in the front row of the plane?"

"Yes." I'm sitting by the window, and I slide down in my seat so I can't see him.

"The gorgeous one with the gray suit and the sexy hair?" Lucy asks.

"Yep." That about sums him up.

"And let me just clarify—the guy's loaded? Like, super rich?"

"Yep." Actually, he's a billionaire, but I'm not about to tell Lucy that. I'm not sure the flight attendants would appreciate a passenger spontaneously combusting.

"And you dumped him?" Lucy's eyes practically bulge onto her cheeks. "What are you, nuts?"

Against my will, I give a short laugh. I hadn't meant to tell her, but the gasp of recognition had burst forth from me as he'd passed us to reach his seat, and she'd demanded to know who he was. "You don't know the whole story," I reply, but I can see she isn't listening.

"I'd give my left arm to date someone like him," she says dreamily. "Honestly, Victoria, sometimes I think you're a sausage short of a barbie. Why did you break up with him?"

"I don't want to talk about it." I open the in-flight magazine and study the article on the fruity red wines from the Marlborough region of the South Island of New Zealand as if it's the most interesting thing I've ever read.

She sighs, but she doesn't press me, and my gaze drifts out of the window to the stunning view. We've only just taken off, and Fiji lies behind us. We have three hours before we land in Auckland, all of which we'll spend over water. The sun is setting to the west above the vast expanse of the Pacific, turning the sea to molten copper. So much empty ocean, all that dark water, filled with sharks and whales and those fish with the scary teeth and the lights on the end of their noses. I don't like to think about it.

On the horizon, the sky is heavy with ominous clouds. I blink as lightning flashes. Great. Flying through a storm—just what the doctor ordered.

Unbidden, my gaze slides to the guy sitting at the front of business class. Theo Prince stretches out his long legs as he watches something on his in-flight screen. Of all the people to be on this plane… Still, he was late to board, and I don't think he saw me as he passed our seats, so hopefully I'll make it to Auckland without him even realizing I'm on the plane.

Lucy takes her laptop out of her backpack and opens it up. "I'm going to run through your schedule for the next week and make sure I've booked everything. Anything you want to add to it?"

"Not at the moment."

She nods and starts tapping on the keyboard.

She's only been my business manager at Wanderlust Yoga for three weeks. My partner-in-crime and best friend Beth declared she needed some help running the company, and so she's now handed over some of the organizational duties so she can concentrate on the big-picture stuff. When Beth hired Lucy to replace her, I'm sure she thought she'd drive me nuts within days. It's true she's a chatterbox and says whatever's on her mind the moment it enters it. I like her, though; her youth and energy have given me a lift while I'm feeling low. But she has yet to work out when I want to talk and when I need peace and quiet, like now.

What I really need is a couple of weeks off to recharge, but that's not going to happen anytime soon. Glancing at Lucy's screen, I can see that the next few months are jam-packed with appointments, interviews, and appearances, squashed around the precious hour a day when I actually get to do any yoga.

I'm not going to bemoan my fame. This was what I wanted, and I've worked hard to get here. I've achieved everything I set out to do, so I can hardly sit here and wish it all away. But as I look out at the darkening sky, I know I've lost a little of my infamous serenity lately.

Of course, that's mostly to do with breaking up with Jack. I defy any woman to remain calm and tranquil with a man like that. At first, his energy and volatility were what attracted me. It's like my life had been filled with pastel colors, and Jack burst into it in a blaze of bright oranges and reds and vivid purples, setting me on fire. I thought I hungered for that passion and vitality, but I didn't know how exhausting it would be to be around someone like that all the time.

And now he's gone, and I want to return to the pastel colors, to the blues and greens and pretty pinks. But at the moment it's as if the colors are pieces of plasticine blended together to make a muddy brown. It's only been six months since he moved out, but I can't find my balance. I'm like a kite whose string has broken, and I'm being tossed about by the wind, rising higher and higher into the clouds.

"Victoria?"

My head snaps around, and I look up at Theo Prince, who's standing in the aisle, staring at me.

Damn it.

"Hey," I reply flatly. My heart taps a rapid tattoo on my ribs. He must be thirty now. Seven years ago, he'd played rugby and football in the winter, tennis and cricket in the summer, and he'd swum all year round, so he'd been lean and muscular. He's filled out over the years, so he has a man's build now, and I think he's grown an inch or two as well. There are fine lines at the corners of his eyes and mouth, but they haven't detracted from his good looks; if anything they've added to it, wiping away the boyishness and instead replacing it with a man's suave handsomeness.

Damn, damn, damn. Why can't he have grown warts and buck teeth and put on a hundred pounds?

My fingers itch to pull out my phone, take a photo, and post it on my Insta account. It would have thousands of likes and a couple of hundred comments in an hour, so at least I'd have gotten something out of our meeting. Unfortunately, though, there's no Wi-Fi on board.

"I didn't realize you were on the plane," he says.

"That's because you were late boarding," I point out. We'd all had to wait for him, and he'd been the last one on.

"True. Sorry about that. I didn't realize I was going to be on the flight until the last minute."

Typical. Disorganized and thinks the whole world is here to wait on him hand and foot. Theo Prince needs a flight—everybody hold their horses!

Lucy clears her throat, and I give her a wry look before saying, "Lucy, this is Theo Prince. Theo, Lucy Rippon, my business manager."

"Pleased to meet you, Lucy," he says, holding out a hand.

"Likewise, Theo." Managing to inject a less-than-subtle sensuality into his name, she slips her hand into his, looking up at him and fluttering her eyelashes. I feel a flash of irritation, although I have no idea why. Why should I care if she finds him attractive?

I wait for him to grin and flirt with her, but although he smiles politely, his gaze slides back to me as he leans on the overhead locker, his shirt sleeves tightening on his biceps. "I was just going to get a drink at the bar," he says. "I don't suppose you'd care to join me?"

At any other time, my answer would have been a sharp no. It might have been a long time since we broke up, but my resentment is hot enough that the last thing I want to do is spend time in his company.

However, I'm conscious that Lucy is probably hoping I'll say no so he'll ask her instead, and my mischievousness flares into life as I find myself saying, "Sure."

Surprise flickers on his face—he'd expected me to refuse, but he smiles and moves back, so I rise from my seat and squeeze past Lucy.

We're in business class as there's no first class on these smaller planes to Fiji. It's a lot roomier than economy, but it's hardly palatial, and he hasn't moved back that far, so I bump into him as I enter the aisle. He's still leaning on the overhead locker, and I have to look up to meet his eyes. Only then do I remember how blue they are.

I clear my throat, turn, and make my way down the aisle to the bar at the back. It's just a small half-circle against an inner wall, but it houses bottles of every drink I could imagine, and the bartender smiles as we approach.

"Can I have a gin and tonic?" I ask.

The bartender nods and begins to mix the drink.

Theo leans on the bar beside me, his eyebrows rising. "You drink alcohol now?"

Back when we were together, I was teetotal, so I understand why he's surprised. "I don't drink much. Just when I feel the need."

"And why do you feel the need now? Not because of seeing me, I hope?"

Yes, that's completely the reason why. I need to slow my heart down before I have a coronary.

"Not at all," I say in what I hope is a nonchalant, you-mean-nothing-to-me-manner. "A G&T dulls the stream of my companion's constant chatter." He laughs, but I feel a twinge of guilt at the comment. "Sorry, that was bitchy of me. She's just started as my business manager. She's excellent at her job and she's very friendly, but she's only been with me for three weeks, so we're not quite fitting together yet."

"What happened to your previous business manager? I'll have a Glenfiddich on the rocks, please," he adds to the bartender as he slides my G&T over to me.

"She's dropping some of the organizational work," I explain. "She deserves to take it a bit easier. She's worked very hard since we started the company."

He obviously realizes to whom I'm referring. "Beth?"

I nod.

He doesn't say anything, and his expression stays blank. I'm not surprised. He and Beth never really got on, and after what happened, I can't imagine his feelings for her improved.

He waits for his drink, then gestures to two seats facing each other across a small table, and we go over and sit.

Outside, rain has started to pepper the glass. Inside, though, it's warm and cozy. Theo leans back and sips his whisky, then places the glass on the table and turns it in his fingers. I wait for him to talk about what happened back then, but instead he says, "I have to say congratulations. You've done incredibly well for yourself."

For a fleeting second, I think he's referring to me meeting Jack, or maybe to me breaking up with him, I'm not sure which. "What do you mean?"

"Wanderlust Yoga," he says, amused. "Nine million subscribers on YouTube, two million on Insta, half a million followers on Facebook. You're on the front cover of every woman's magazine in Australasia, the star of the show on the Rise and Shine TV program. Five books published, your own range of yoga clothing and beauty products. Appearances all over New Zealand, Australia, and the Pacific Islands. Do you ever have time to sleep?"

I'm shocked, and immensely flattered that he's been aware of my journey, although I try not to look it. "Luckily, I only need four or five hours."

"Yeah," he says, "I remember."

Our eyes meet, and for a moment I can't breathe. I'm transported right back to those lazy Sunday mornings in his apartment, where we'd stay in bed until lunchtime, eating croissants and making love for hours as the sun rose slowly in the sky.

"I'll always remember you standing outside on the balcony," he says, "doing the sun salutation naked at sunrise." His smile is an arrow straight to my heart, lacking none of the speed or strength to affect me as it did when I first met him.

I look down at my drink. I don't want to think about how glorious it was back then. It's like remembering how bright and hot the sun was while you were on vacation, when you're at home and it's raining every day and so cold you have to wear sweaters indoors.

It was an age ago, and I've long since stopped crying over Theo Prince.

"Sorry," he says. "I didn't mean to make you sad."

"I'm not sad. As you said, I'm doing great."

"Maybe it's just me, then."

I look back up at him. It's true, he does look sad. For the first time, I notice the dark shadows under his eyes. He looks tired and somewhat dispirited.

"What were you doing in Fiji?" I ask. "I'm guessing you're working for the family business?" I don't really have to ask; I've looked him up from time to time over the years too, so I know he's the Marketing Director for Prince's Toy Store. Started by one of his relatives back in England in the nineteenth century, the business has grown over the past one hundred and fifty years to become an international phenomenon, with stores all over Europe, Australia, and New Zealand, and recently a couple in the States, too. As Marketing Director, Theo would probably be in charge of the business's presence online, which would be why he's so comfortable with Instagram and Facebook and the like.

"I was the keynote speaker at a business conference," he replies.

It doesn't surprise me. He's also the face of the company, the one most likely to appear in interviews or articles. One of the Sunday papers did a big spread on the family only a few weeks ago after the opening of their new theme park, The South Pole. They had older photos of Nick, Theo's Dad, and Richard, his grandfather, but it was Theo who gave the interview, and who talked about not only the success of the business, but also of the tragedies that had befallen the family over the past few years.

"I was sorry to hear about your mum," I say. "She was a lovely woman." Olivia Prince had been spirited and fun, and we'd gotten on well for the six months Theo and I had dated.

"Thanks. Yes, that came as a shock. A brain aneurysm. Very sudden."

"That's awful. And I'm sorry to hear about Ben's wife, too." His older brother lost his wife in a car accident. She was nine months pregnant, but luckily they were able to save the baby. He dips his head in acknowledgement. "And how's your grandfather doing?" I ask. The article stated that Richard Prince had a brain tumor, and he'd had to step down as CEO.

Theo studies his glass and swirls the whisky over the ice. "Actually, he died this morning."

My jaw drops. "Oh, Theo, no. I'm so sorry."

"I only got the call a few hours ago. Initially they'd said he probably wouldn't make Christmas, but he'd picked up a little over the past couple of weeks, and we were hoping he'd see the New Year. It's the only reason why I agreed to go to Fiji. But he took a sudden turn for the worse last night, and this morning he was gone. I should have flown home last night, but I was tired after the conference, so I thought I'd wait until morning. I'll never forgive myself for that."

He stops talking, and I watch emotion wash over him as if he's lying on the beach and a wave has rolled up the sand. He lifts a hand and rests his lips on his knuckles, clearly fighting for control. I feel helpless. I'm not his wife or his girlfriend; we're not even friends, not now, and anyway there's nothing I can say that will make things better. I know he loved the old man.

So I do the only thing I can—I reach out a hand and rest it on his where he's holding the glass. He turns his over, and our fingers curl around each other's and tighten.

His hands are strong and brown, his nails short and neat. I can remember that hand on my breast, looking so tanned against my white skin. He had a thousand ways to kiss me, from gentle as a butterfly landing on my lips to a thousand-watt-crush of his lips to mine. No man has matched up to him since, not even Jack, whose lovemaking was passionate, and enthusiastic, for want of a better word.

But Theo broke my heart, and he didn't just break it in a simple crack down the middle, but he shattered it into a thousand pieces, like a broken glass where the shards scatter across the room and disappear under cupboards and down drains. I know I'll never get them all back.

I'll never love another man the way I loved him. But it was a long time ago, and I have to make sure he stays firmly in the past where he belongs.

Chapter Two

Theo

The grief that crashes over me is sudden and fierce, making me clench my teeth hard so I don't break down, and it takes a good thirty seconds before it releases its grip.

If I was on my own, I'd have happily given in to my sorrow, but not only am I on a plane with people passing by, I'm also sitting opposite Victoria Sullivan, and the last thing I want to do is crumble in front of the one woman I want to impress more than any other.

I couldn't believe it when I glanced across the seats and saw her sitting there. At first I thought I was imagining her. Lord knows she flits through my mind most days, like a ghost in white through the hallways of a stately home. But I blinked and she was still there, so I knew she must be real, with her slender, toned body, glossy hair the color of sunlight on sand, big hazel eyes, a thin top lip and a plump bottom lip that begs to be kissed, and the wonderful, cute dimples in her cheeks.

I haven't seen her in person for seven years, but I have followed her online, so I wasn't surprised to see the hair she used to wear loose now up in a scruffy bun, a few fine lines at the corner of her eyes, and of course the scar on her left cheekbone from the accident she had six months ago. It's not as red and raw as it was in the photo I saw, snapped by a journalist as she came out of the hospital, but it's still pink and noticeable.

Even though I've kept an eye on her over the years, it's not the same as being face to face, and it's only when she joined me for a drink that I saw the changes weren't just superficial. When we were together, she was only twenty-one, and she had a *joie de vivre* I adored, a lightness of soul that's one of the reasons people must follow her. But I spotted a thread on Twitter just a month or so ago where her fans were discussing how her accident seemed to have affected her enthusiasm in her videos. I dismissed it, because the Internet is full of all kinds of crazy but, looking into her eyes, I fail to find her infamous sparkle, as if someone has blown out her pilot light.

Gradually, the wave of grief subsides, and I lower my hand and blow out a long breath. "Sorry about that. It hit me like a cartoon frying pan."

Her lips curve up, but she doesn't remove the hand that's resting on mine. "You always did love Tom and Jerry."

"Still do."

"I am sorry," she insists, squeezing my fingers. "I bet you'll be glad to get back home to your family. You were always tight."

"Yeah, that hasn't changed."

She finally releases my hand and picks up her drink. "So… will Emma be waiting on the tarmac when you touch down?"

My heart skips a beat as I realize she's followed me online, too. I don't react, though, and instead just say, "No. We broke up."

"Oh." I can tell by her reaction that she knew. "You'd been dating her for a while, hadn't you?" She clears her throat then, obviously realizing she's revealed she's followed me. "There was a feature on the new theme park on Rise and Shine a while ago."

"Yeah, we'd been together a couple of years."

"It didn't work out?"

I shake my head. I don't want to talk to her about Emma.

One of the flight attendants is making her way down the aisle, and she approaches us and smiles. "The captain has put the seatbelt sign on, so would you mind…" She gestures at our belts.

"Of course." I buckle up, and Victoria does the same. She's wearing a white T-shirt over a pair of black leggings. Neutral colors; she wants to hide from the world.

As the attendant walks away, Victoria ducks her head and looks out of the window. "There's a storm brewing. I hope it's not coming this way."

I follow her gaze and watch lightning illuminate the sea in the distance. Rain lashes against the window, and we hear the rolling boom of thunder, audible even over the roar of the plane's engines. I shiver.

"Are you cold?" she asks.

"No. Someone walked over my grave."

Her eyes meet mine. "You haven't gotten one of your feelings, have you?"

I'm touched she remembers. Sometimes I get a strange prickle on the back of my neck, as if someone's trying to tell me to take note of something. I rarely speak of my odd sixth sense to anyone outside the family. I told Victoria a few weeks after we started dating, but I never told Emma. Funny, that.

"A bit," I reply, because I don't want to tell her that I'm filled with a sense of unease so strong my heart is starting to race.

She looks back out of the window, frowning. I pull out my phone, bring up my texts, and compose one quickly to the family group that includes my father and my siblings. *Love you all. I'll be home soon. T xx* There's no Wi-Fi on the plane, but I send it anyway. It might catch a passing wave and get through.

I put the phone on the table. Victoria is watching me. "Now I'm nervous," she admits.

"I'm sure we'll be fine. So, why were you in Fiji? Were you doing a program for Wanderlust?"

"Yes, a series actually." She finishes off her G&T with a gulp. "I don't know if you remember, but with Wanderlust our idea was to blend yoga with travel. We've recorded videos in front of the Eiffel Tower, in Trafalgar Square in London, at the Grand Canyon, that kind of thing. Beth thought a series set on a tropical beach would be appealing."

"I can see that being very popular."

"My fans are looking forward to it."

I smile. "I told you you'd be famous."

She opens her mouth to reply, but at that moment the speaker crackles and the captain starts talking. He informs us a storm has blown up to the west and we're going to experience some turbulence, so we should keep our seatbelts on for a while.

"Maybe we should go back to our seats," Victoria suggests.

I have a very strong feeling we should stay where we are. "We're all right here," I tell her, fighting against rising anxiety.

She nods, only half listening, and I know she's thinking about what I said regarding knowing she'd be famous when she continues, "Beth's always said the same. I wouldn't have done half the things I have without her believing in me."

11

I sit back in the chair and finish off my whisky. I like to think I'm an amiable guy. It's one reason why the family suggested I do most of the interviews for the company—I can charm most people, and it's rare for me not to get on with anyone as I tend to find something to like in everyone. I can count on one hand the number of people I dislike.

And I can count on one finger the number I hate.

"And how is Beth?" I say. I'm not surprised to hear that my voice has turned to ice. I am shocked at how fresh the hate feels, as if it all happened yesterday.

Victoria scans my face, and her smile fades. "Even after all this time?" she whispers. "You still can't let it go?"

I can think of a hundred ways to reply to that comment, but I know none of them will express the depth of the anger and resentment I will always bear toward her best friend. And the last thing I want to do is sour the mood, even though her words have caused the flare of hope I felt when I met her to fade. This isn't going to be a second chance for us. There won't be any happy ending, not all the time Beth Richards is still part of Victoria's life, because her presence means Victoria still blames me. If I couldn't change that seven years ago, how on earth am I going to change it now?

I'm distracted by a flash outside the window, and we both look out to see lightning tear the sky apart. It's close—too close—and it hits the tip of the wing.

I know it's extremely rare for lightning to cause problems with planes. They're made to withstand electrical storms, and usually the lightning passes through the conductive outer shell of the aircraft.

But this time, something goes wrong. There's a boom and the airplane shakes, and a fraction of a second later there's a massive explosion. We both swear loudly, and we stare in horror as fire erupts on the wing.

"It's hit the fuel tank," I say. "We're in trouble, Vic."

After this, everything happens quickly, and there's no time to think. The oxygen masks drop at the same time as the captain's voice comes on the speaker, telling everyone to assume crash positions. Pandemonium erupts in the cabin, people yelling or crying. The flight attendants go from seat to seat telling everyone to put on their life jackets and oxygen masks, trying to keep everyone calm, but it's a pointless exercise.

We're not in our proper seats, but we put on the masks anyway.

"Theo," Victoria says, her voice muffled behind the mask. Her eyes are wide, terrified. "Are we going to die?"

"We won't, I promise." I don't know if it's my sixth sense speaking or if I'm trying to stop us panicking.

Screams echo from the economy section, and I go cold. There are children there. This is horrific. I want to help, but the plane is descending rapidly, and it's all I can do to sit upright and hang onto the table.

Victoria's hand finds mine, and we clutch together as the plane crashes into the sea. My last sane thought is of the text I typed, and that I hope it found its way to my family.

*

A jumble of images, sounds, and screams.

Flickering lights that suddenly go out.

More screams and sobs.

Amazingly, Victoria and I are unharmed, with little more than bangs and bruises. But we're now stuck in a metal box that's gradually sinking into the cold sea. Things aren't looking good.

The emergency lighting is an eerie strip leading passengers down the aisle to the emergency doors. We help a flight attendant remove the door by the toilets. The attendant has blood all over her forehead, but she continues regardless.

Icy-cold water spills into the cabin. I'm ankle deep, and it's rising so fast I find it difficult to tear my gaze away from it.

In their panic, some people can't get their seat belts undone. I help those nearest to us, but people are scrambling for the doors, blocking the aisles. I can see Lucy Rippon in her seat, sobbing, but I can't get down the aisle. The flight attendant pushes a couple of life rafts out and they inflate. Lightning flashes in the sky, and terror slices through me at the sight of the huge waves lifting the rafts high into the air before they plummet down again. It also illuminates Victoria's face, which is white as the moon.

The sounds are deafening—not just from the passengers, but also the scream and groan of twisted metal. The plane is a giant animal, a leviathan going down, fighting to stay alive.

"Go," the attendant snaps. "Get out while you can."

I look over my shoulder. There are still people in the cabin, and Lucy is crying in her seat.

"If you stay," the attendant says, "you'll die."

I want to save Lucy. But more than that, I want to live. And I want Victoria to live.

I grab her hand and pull her with me over the debris littering the floor of the plane. The water is up to my chest now. We heave ourselves through the doorway. I have a glimpse of the flight attendant's face, her big green eyes lit up by the lightning, before a huge wave washes over us and blocks out the scene.

I'm still holding Victoria's hand. With my left, I flounder and grasp rope, and I pull Victoria up so she's holding it too. The waves rise until it feels we're on top of a mountain. Lightning flashes, and I can see the plane, bubbles rising as it sinks into the inky depths. There are half a dozen other rafts bobbing like corks. I can see only a dozen or so people in them.

It takes every ounce of strength I own to clamber into the raft. I lean over and pull Victoria up too, and she falls in beside me. I need to help everyone else. I blow the whistle on my life jacket and lean over, looking for hands to grab, but I can't see anything, and nobody takes my hand.

The rain hammers down—heavy, torrential, sub-tropical rain, hanging between the raft and the scene before me like a thick curtain. It's impossible to see anything. I wait for the lightning to flash again, but when it does, there's only black water; I can't even see the other rafts. The plane has gone. I think of the flight attendant with the green eyes, the older man who sat next to me on the plane, of Lucy with her bubbly brown hair and flirtatious eyes.

Turning, I fall back into the bottom of the raft. Victoria is curled in a ball, crying. I wrap my arms around her, doing my best to shield her from the rain, but it's impossible. We're lying in a foot of water, and we're both frozen.

We can't do anything but ride this out. It must be about midnight, so it's going to be a long time before the sun rises. God knows where we are. Somewhere between Fiji and New Zealand. I know Fiji consists of about three hundred and thirty islands and another five hundred or so islets or tiny islands. But the Pacific is vast, and empty, and deep. I don't know what the chances are of us striking land, but I wouldn't bet my house on it.

Victoria turns over in the boat to face me, tucking her head under my chin. I tighten my arms, shivering, and rub her back, trying to keep her warm.

"Theo…" she sobs. "Oh my God…"

"I know…" Thunder drowns out my reply. I hold her so tightly I'm in danger of cracking her ribs, but she doesn't complain, so I don't let go.

There are sharks in the Pacific, and crocodiles, and box jellyfish, and probably several thousand other creatures that could kill us.

But we're alive. And now we just have to wait for the sun to come up.

Chapter Three

Victoria

When I wake, it's daylight. It's still raining, the drops pinging off the rubber dinghy, and surprisingly loud on the surface of the ocean.

I'm lying in about six inches of water, and I'm freezing. My eyes feel gritty, and they sting as I force them open.

There's only one other person with me. Theo is sitting up, shading his eyes from the rain as he scans the ocean. It all comes rushing back to me then—the lightning strike, the crash, swimming out through the emergency door to the surface, and then Theo hauling me up into the dinghy. I must have passed out, because I can only vaguely remember rising and falling with the huge waves, and Theo curled around me, his arms holding me tightly.

"Hey," I say. My voice sounds hoarse. I seem to remember crying for half the night. I kept thinking about Lucy and the other people who didn't manage to escape, and I'd been convinced I was going to die. I've never been so terrified. I can vaguely remember Theo telling me over and over again that everything was going to be all right and rubbing my back to keep me warm.

He turns his head, relief in his eyes. "You're awake."

"I don't know if I fell asleep or fainted. I'm sorry."

He looks back out to sea. "The storm seems to have passed. The waves aren't as high, and the lightning has stopped."

"Can you see the other boats? Any people?"

"No. The sun's behind the clouds in that direction, so we're drifting… ah… south-west, I think. But I have no idea where we are."

"We're in the middle of the Pacific."

A ghost of a smile appears on his lips. "True."

I brush a hand over my face. "I'm thirsty."

"Don't drink the water in the bottom. It's mixed with sea water. Here, hold your hands like this." He cups them, and I copy him. They gradually fill with rainwater, and after a minute or two I'm able to quench my thirst.

"Don't suppose you've got a KitKat in your pocket," I joke.

"Unfortunately not." He slides his hands into the pockets of his trousers and extracts a soggy serviette from one, and his wallet from the other. He flips it open. "Credit cards, for all the good they'll do. Seventy-five bucks and a couple of coins." He pulls out a small square packet and lets it unfold to reveal three condoms. His eyes raise to meet mine.

"Don't even think about it," I say.

He returns them to his wallet and slides it back into his trousers. "When we find our desert island, we're going to have to repopulate it, so we won't need them anyway."

"Don't make me laugh. It's not funny."

"No, it's not."

We study each other quietly for a while, listening to the rain.

"Have you got your phone?" I ask eventually.

He shakes his head. "I left it on the table. You?"

"I don't have anything. My phone was in the pocket by my seat." I feel a sharp sense of something approaching panic at the thought of being without my phone. It spends a good part of the day either in my hand or less than a foot away from me. I'm constantly texting, emailing, checking Insta or Facebook or Snapchat or Twitter or TikTok, taking photos or videos, or listening to music. The most important thing in my life currently lies at the bottom of the ocean. I have a vision of one of the fish with the big teeth watching a video of a cat falling into a waste-paper basket. I give a semi-hysterical laugh and cut it off quickly as Theo's eyebrows rise.

"I think I'm hallucinating," I tell him.

He sighs, looks at the water in the bottom of the dinghy, and begins to scoop it up in his hands and throw it overboard.

His hair is plastered to his head, and he has a day's growth of stubble. I've never seen him with a beard; he was always very well-groomed. He's still wearing his life jacket. His white shirt has popped a couple of buttons and is held together by just two in the middle and his tie, which he's still wearing. His trousers are clinging to his legs. He's still wearing his smart lace-up brogues.

I look down at myself. My T-shirt and leggings are intact beneath my life jacket. My jandals have vanished though, and my feet are red with cold.

"I'm glad my fans can't see me now," I comment.

"You look amazing," he replies.

"You're trying to be nice," I say wryly. "I bet I look frightful."

"You do, a bit. But you're still the most beautiful woman I've ever seen." He says it casually, while continuing to scoop out the water. I know he doesn't mean it, but I appreciate his attempt to make me feel better.

My spirits remain low, though, panic and fear churning around in my stomach. "What are we going to do?" I whisper. "We're really screwed, aren't we?"

He stops scooping for a second, then carries on. I turn onto my knees and start helping him.

"We're likely to drift to land eventually," he says. "It's the way the tides work. There are hundreds of islands around here."

"How long can we go without food and water?"

"A month without food. Only three days without water. We're all right as long as it's raining. It'll be more of a problem once the sun comes out."

I sit up and look up into the sky, shading my eyes from the rain. I can't imagine ever seeing the sun again. "What's the likelihood of us being spotted by a plane?"

"Not great like this, I wouldn't think. If we can get to land and build a signal fire, they'll find us."

"You sound more confident than I feel."

He stops scooping and sits back down. "My family will come looking for me. Dad won't stop until he finds me."

"So if I stick with you, I should be okay?"

His lips twitch. "Your fans will raise a fortune to pay for someone to rescue you. It's going to be all over the Internet. They'll start a GoFundMe account, rescue you, and leave me there."

I feel too dispirited to laugh. "I wonder how many people made it out of the plane."

"There weren't many in the other dinghies. A dozen, maybe."

"And how many on board? A couple of hundred?" He nods. Tears prick my eyes. "That's so awful. There were children on there. I heard them crying." I bite my lip hard, thinking of Lucy. So young, so full of life. "We should have done more."

"If we'd stayed, we would have died. The flight attendant told me that." He looks away.

We're quiet for a while. The rain patters on the rubber and the ocean. I lean my head on the side, wrapping my arms around me, trying not to shiver, and failing.

"Are there sharks here?" I whisper.

His gaze comes back to me. "Don't think about it."

But it's impossible not to.

Until my car crash, I never really thought about death. I was ill as a child with chickenpox, but I never came close to dying, and I haven't had a serious illness since. I'm not particularly a thrill seeker, so I've never bungee jumped or paraglided or anything.

When Jack lost control of the Mercedes and it spun across the motorway and into the barrier, I knew it was bad. The firefighters had to cut me out of the car, and there was blood everywhere. I was very lucky not to break anything. But the second after the crunch of metal meeting metal, I knew I'd survived it.

Now, though, I'm not so sure. People could search for us every day from dawn until dusk, but the Pacific is a vast ocean. Maybe the storm had blown the plane off its flight plan. We could drift for days and be hundreds of miles from where the plane crashed.

We might never be found.

We could end up on a tiny islet and die from an injury, or be eaten by sharks or crocodiles.

Or we could die from hunger, or more likely thirst, right here in this dinghy.

A tear runs down my face, but it's lost in the rain. Somehow Theo still notices, though, and says, "Don't cry."

"I don't want to die," I say softly.

"Me neither. I have every intention of getting to that island and getting started on the repopulation."

I sniff, knowing he's trying to cheer me up. "If we have to resort to cannibalism, I'm going to start with your knob. Fried up, it'll be like having one of those giant hot dogs."

That makes him laugh, even though there's nothing remotely funny about our situation.

It's impossible to avoid a pressing need, though, and eventually I admit, "I need to pee."

"More difficult for you than for me," he admits. "You'll have to stick your butt over the edge."

"I'm not doing that."

"You're going to pee in the raft?"

I hesitate, realizing I don't have an option. "I've changed my mind. I don't need to go."

"I'll hold onto your hands," he promises.

Oh, is this real? I can't bear for my ex to watch me pee out of a boat. But what choice do I have?

"Only if you close your eyes." I wait until he dutifully closes them before lowering my leggings and panties. "Man, this is embarrassing."

"We're going to have to get used to a lot worse than this," he says, holding out his hands as I maneuver myself to the edge. There follows a few minutes of us trying to keep our balance while I lower myself down enough so I don't pee into the dinghy.

"Done?" he asks.

"Hold on. I'm terrified a shark's going to bite my bum."

"Don't make me laugh. I don't want to drop you."

When I'm done, I let him pull me back, and quickly tug up my panties and leggings. "Don't say a word."

"Wouldn't dream of it." He's trying not to smile. "Want a hug?"

"No."

"You look cold. It might help to share some body heat."

I don't want to be stuck in a boat with only Theo for company. It's so painful to be near him, I just want to sob. But there are more important things right now than my broken heart—staying alive, for one.

"You promise not to feel me up?" I ask.

"No."

"I'm a black belt in Jiu Jitsu now," I say as I scoot across. The dinghy dips, so we adjust our weight until it levels, then cuddle up together.

"Duly warned," he replies, pulling me close to his chest.

I tuck my head under his chin, curling up as much as I can, glad of his warmth in spite of myself. "Of all the people," I murmur.

"What?"

"Of all the people in the world to be stuck here with, I end up with you, Theo Prince."

"I bet you didn't realize you were such a lucky person."

"Actually I was cursing my misfortune."

"Yeah. Me too." His arms tighten around me.

It's a jest, of course. I could have ended up here alone, or with a stranger, or even worse with a man who wasn't as decent as Theo.

It's a strange word to pick. I seem to remember having a colorful collection of insults for him seven years ago. I called him all the names under the sun.

I don't want to think about it now. I close my eyes and let the rise and dip of the boat lull me into a dreamless sleep.

*

We drift all morning, and then in the afternoon the rain stops, the clouds clear, and the sun comes out. Within half an hour, our clothes and hair are dry, and it's incredibly hot.

It's a relief not to be soaked to the skin, but I know the fine weather will cause us a lot more problems. There's no drinking water, and it doesn't take long for my lips to feel dry and my throat parched. I've always been good at protecting my skin from the hot Kiwi sun, and there's nowhere to hide, so I'm sure we're both going to get horribly sunburned.

Theo takes off his life jacket and tie, and removes his shirt before replacing the life jacket. He soaks the shirt in the sea, and we both lie in the bottom of the dinghy with it over our faces to keep us cool.

Normally it would be a struggle not to stare at his naked skin and his muscles, but I feel faint from hunger and permanently terrified, so sex is the last thing on my mind.

We don't talk much. It makes my mouth too dry. Instead we doze, and rouse, doze, and rouse, occasionally lifting our heads to check the horizon, then lowering back down when we find only ocean and sky.

As the sun sets, it gets cold again. Theo puts his shirt back on, and we huddle back together once more for warmth. I feel lethargic and a bit dizzy. I normally drink a lot, eight glasses of water a day plus several herbal teas and my one guilty coffee in the morning.

"I'd kill for a cup of tea," I murmur.

He kisses the top of my head. "I was just thinking the same. With a bacon sandwich." His voice has turned husky. I'd find it attractive if I didn't know he was dehydrated.

"Oh, yes. With thick butter and ketchup."

"I thought you were a vegetarian."

"I am, but right now I could eat a horse."

He gives a short laugh. "I've never understood how anyone could give up meat. Juicy steaks, sizzling sausages, roast lamb with mint sauce…"

"I'd be happy for some pasta with cheese," I whisper, "a fresh green salad, and a glass of white wine."

"A double whisky over ice for me."

"Mm. Or a long glass of iced tea."

Theo's quiet for a while. Then he says, "Do you still like croissants?"

He's thinking about our Sunday mornings in bed. "With strawberry jam," I reply.

"And peanut butter."

"Crunchy."

"Smooth," he corrects. We both give a small laugh. "Those were good days," he says.

My eyes fill with tears. "Don't."

He gives a long, heartfelt sigh, and doesn't speak again for a while.

Feeling stiff, I shift onto my back and join him in looking up at the stars as they begin to appear in the black velvet sky.

"So many of them," I whisper.

"Do you know anything about astronomy?"

"Nothing at all. I can just about find the moon." I gesture to the silver orb, about three-quarters full.

So he begins to point things out to me—the Milky Way, which is like a splash of milk across the sky to the south, the Crux or Southern Cross, with its sparkly Jewel Box cluster of stars, and, as the dinghy turns slowly to face north-east, Orion's Belt, from which he traces a line to Sirius, the dog star.

"The brightest star you can see in the southern hemisphere," he says. He lowers his arm with a thump, clearly lacking the strength to keep it raised for long.

I turn onto my side facing away from him, and he curls up around me. "How do you know so much about them?" I ask.

"My granddad. He had a telescope, and he taught us all about the stars. He was a Scout leader."

"Oh, really?"

"We all joined when we were young—Keas, they called us, until the age of eight, then we became Cubs until we were eleven. The others left after that, but I enjoyed the outdoor life, and I was a Scout until I was fourteen."

"So you know your knots?"

"Oh yes. Once, Granddad took all of us—me, Ben, Lucas, Jacob, and Kora—out into the bush for two whole nights and taught us survival skills."

"So if we do land on an island, we'll have no problem."

"No problem at all."

We both fall quiet again, watching the stars wheel overhead as the dinghy slowly turns. Theo sighs, and I know he must be thinking about his grandfather. His family will be distraught to have lost Theo too.

Dad won't stop until he finds me. I wonder if he just said that to reassure me, or if he really believes it. And even if he really believes it, how true is it? How likely is it that someone will find us? There's no way of knowing.

My own father probably won't even realize I'm missing. The thought makes me very sad.

The dinghy bobs and turns, the lapping waves the only sound in the night.

Chapter Four

Theo

The next day is a repeat of the previous. We bob and spin in the ocean, baking slowly under the hot summer sun.

In the morning, we're too dehydrated to do anything other than lie there under my soaked shirt. Most of the time we doze, rousing only to re-wet the shirt and check the horizon before lying back down again.

When the sun is high in the sky, we're blessed with a light shower for a couple of hours, and we spend most of the time with our hands out, drinking as much as we can. I'm hopeful that the rain means we must be near land, because doesn't water condense over land to form rain? But the horizon remains empty. I can't believe there's so much water. The ocean is an endless carpet of blue, now barely touched by waves.

Refreshed by our drink, we sit up for a while, and we're treated to the sight of a pod of dolphins. They come right up to the dinghy, intent on investigating us, and swim around us for a while.

I observe Victoria's face as she watches them leaping and diving. Her eyes light up, and she even laughs once or twice, her fear forgotten for a while. I need to get her to safety. I have absolute faith that Dad will find us eventually, because I know he'd never allow himself to give up. My only fear is that by the time that happens, we'll have died from dehydration or something even worse. But at the moment there's nothing I can do about it. There's no point in paddling because I don't know in which direction to paddle. Nobody will hear us if we yell. I haven't seen a single plane. All we can do is wait and hope Tangaroa, the Maori god of the sea and fish, takes pity on us.

In the afternoon, buoyed by the presence of the dolphins and the brief shower, we lie in the boat and talk for a while beneath the soaked shirt to distract ourselves from our hunger.

We decide we have to come up with a definitive list of the top fifty movies, and spend what must be at least an hour arguing over the top ten, adding and removing films as we make our case. After that, we talk for a bit about where we've traveled, and which are the most beautiful cities in the world.

But we don't discuss our personal lives. And we don't talk about what happened seven years ago.

I think we're both conscious that our situation is dire, and we're either going to meet a very sticky end, or we might well have to spend some serious time together. And I don't think either of us wants that time to be full of bitterness and regret.

So we talk as if we're strangers, with only the occasional brief reference to the fact that we once knew each other better than anyone else on earth.

As daylight begins to fade, we catch our breaths at the sight of a couple of whale flukes rising out of the sea in the distance.

"What kind are they?" Victoria asks.

"They're orcas."

"Killer whales?"

I nod.

"Do they kill humans?" she asks.

"No. They won't come near us." I cross my fingers that they won't accidentally knock us out of the raft.

"They're so graceful," she whispers as they arc elegantly out of the waves, then send spray shooting up into the air.

"They remind me of you," I tell her.

She laughs. "I'm not sure if that's a compliment."

"It is. When you used to do your yoga, moving through the poses. You always looked so sleek and elegant."

She turns her head and rests her cheek on the edge of the dinghy. I'd promised myself I wouldn't say anything personal, but I couldn't help it.

She meets my eyes, and we study each other for a long while. Will she raise the subject of our past now?

But she turns her head and rests her chin on the rubber. "I miss my phone," she says.

"Yeah, me too." I'd have been texting my family a photo of the orcas right now.

"I feel lonely," she says. "I hadn't realized how comforting I find the connection with all my followers. It's like my consciousness expands and I become part of all of them, but now I'm just me." She sighs.

"Just you is pretty good," I tell her.

But she shakes her head. "I'm empty, Theo. I have been for some time. I've lost my connection with the divine, and I'm not sure I'll ever find it again." She trails a hand in the water.

"I wouldn't do that," I say. "Jellyfish," I add at her querying look, and she snatches her hand back into the boat.

"Why do you feel empty?" I ask. "Was it to do with your ex?"

She doesn't say anything for a while. Then she mumbles, "I don't want to talk about him. Not with you."

I feel the same about Emma, so I don't argue.

She shivers and sits back. "It's so deep and dark down there. It makes me feel funny to think about how far down it goes."

"Victoria…"

"If we were to drown, we could sink miles before we reached the bottom."

"Don't think about it."

"I can't help it. I don't want to die out here." Her eyes are wide, her chest rising and falling rapidly with panic. "I don't want to lie like a shipwreck on the bottom of the ocean, covered in barnacles. I like breathing."

"We'll be okay…"

"You don't know that. You can't know that. There's no sign of land. We could drift for weeks, months. You said we can only survive for three days without water."

"I know…"

"Maybe we should just jump in now and let the sea have us. I don't want to draw it out over days. I think I'd rather get it over and done with. It's like suffocating, right? It wouldn't last long, just a couple of minutes, and then it'd all be done…"

"Stop it!"

She blinks, and then her eyes fill with tears.

"We'll be all right," I say softly. "I promise."

"You can't promise that…"

"I just know we're going to be fine. Trust me."

She shivers, wrapping her arms around her waist. The sun is going down, and the temperature is dropping. "Your sixth sense?"

"My sixth sense. You're going to have to trust me."

Even as I say the words, I realize the irony of them. Because trusting me was the one thing she couldn't do all those years ago.

But this time she gives a nod, and she lets me lead her to the middle of the raft and pull her into my arms. She's five-nine, tallish for a woman, but she feels tiny and fragile, even though I've always thought of her as strong.

"Sing to me," she whispers.

My throat is parched, my lips are dry and cracking, and I'm tired. But I sing her 'You are My Sunshine'. I used to sing it to her all those years ago. But she doesn't complain.

*

We doze through most of the night. Once, a fine spray lands across us, and I hear the mournful call of a sperm whale close by. But we remain untouched, and the stars turn slowly above us, beautiful, cold, and distant at the same time.

*

"Theo!"

I come to with a start, and blink. The raft is bathed in orange light. The sun must be rising, and we've made it through another night.

Victoria isn't lying next to me. She's leaning on the edge of the dinghy. As I rise, the raft bumps against something, hard enough to tell me it's an object and not a wave. And then I hear it—the cry of a seagull.

I scramble to my knees and join her in looking to the east.

"Land," she whispers.

In front of us is a small island, maybe a mile wide. We're resting against a rocky outcrop, about twenty feet from a long sandy beach to our right.

I look at Victoria. Tears are pouring down her face. "You were right," she says, her voice hoarse.

"I told you to trust me," I joke.

She wipes her face, looking back at the island. "Shall we swim?"

"Let's try to paddle. There might be jellyfish around, or sea snakes."

"Sea snakes!"

"There are two or three dangerous ones." I go to the right of the raft, and she moves to the left. I peer over the edge. I can see tiny fish darting around, but there's no sign of anything dangerous. "All right, let's give it a go. Be careful of the coral, too, it can be quite sharp."

We begin to paddle. It's hard work because we're both weak, but excitement gives us some energy, and it's not long before we've skirted the rocks and we can see sand beneath us. Together, we jump out of the raft into the water. It's cool but not icy, the shallow water already warmed by the rising sun, and we half-swim and half-wade onto the beach, pulling the raft with us.

When we reach it, we pull the dinghy up on the sand a little, then collapse back. Oh, the bliss of feeling *terra firma* beneath me. I look up at the bright blue sky, disoriented without the constant rocking of the raft. It'll take a while for that to stop.

"I can't believe we made it," Victoria says, sitting up and looking around. "It doesn't look inhabited."

"No, it's an islet I think, one of the tiny bits of land. But it's better than nothing."

"I'm not complaining. It's the most beautiful place I've ever seen."

I push myself up and turn to look at the place that's going to be our home for the foreseeable future.

It's not huge. The beach is about sixty feet long and twenty feet wide. To our left it turns into chunky rocks and then thick bush. To the front and to the right, palms and trees line ground that rises sharply, culminating in a pointed rock right at the top of the hill.

I unbuckle my life jacket and slide it off, then tug on my shirt to stop my shoulders and back burning. It only has two buttons left in the center, but it's enough to hold it on.

She also removes her jacket. Her white T-shirt is wet and clings tightly to her breasts, revealing her lacy bra. I can't help but notice, even though I'm faint from dehydration and hunger.

"Do you think there are any wild animals here?" she asks.

"I don't think so. The most dangerous creatures are in the sea. We'll have to watch out for crocodiles coming ashore, that's all. There might be rats. A few reptiles and amphibians—frogs, toads, iguanas. Insects, obviously."

"Poisonous ones?"

"No. Huntsman spiders are pretty big, but they're not dangerous."

She swallows hard. "Snakes?"

"No, only in the sea."

"Can we catch malaria?"

"No, the mozzies don't have it here. They might give us dengue fever, but that's about it."

We sit quietly for a while. I don't think either of us can believe we made it.

The island is far from perfect. I can't see any other land nearby. We could be hundreds of miles from Suva, Fiji's capital city. But it's got to be better than floating at sea for weeks.

"I feel so tired," Victoria says. "I guess that's the dehydration. Do we need to look for water first?" She has big dark shadows under her eyes. She tries to remove the elastic band that was holding her hair up in a bun, but soon realizes it's become knotted in the wet strands. "Ouch."

I motion for her to turn around, then start to try to untangle her hair. "The Scouts mnemonic is STOP. Stop, Think, Observe, and Plan. Let's think about it logically. Granddad taught us the five pillars of survival are shelter, water, fire, food, and mindset."

"Mindset?"

"It's important to stay positive and assume we'll be found. Pretty much everything we need will be here. And at least we're not alone." I finally remove the elastic and hold it over her shoulder.

She takes it, and our fingers touch. She pauses, then turns around, and our eyes meet. "I can't imagine how I would've felt if I'd been on my own," she says. She brushes sand off her leggings. "Look, Theo, I think maybe we should make something clear. We're obviously not going to be able to erase what happened between us. But it was seven years ago. I just want to say… I don't bear any ill will toward you. And I'm glad you're here with me." She gives me an expectant smile.

I know I need to tell her how relieved I am that she's here too, but her words make me bristle. Yes, it's been seven years. Over two-and-a-half thousand days. We were so in love, and knew each other so well. Or I thought we did. And yet she still blames me. The hurt and resentment that rushes through me is as fresh and strong as it was back then.

Her smile fades as she obviously reads my expression. The light dies from her eyes, and the shutters come down.

"I shouldn't have said anything," she says. "I'm sorry for bringing it up." She gets to her feet. "I'm going to have a look around."

"Victoria…"

But she's already walking off.

I let her go, lacking the energy for an argument, and not wanting that anyway on our first hour on the island.

She was right to try and explain that she wants us to move on. I should let it go. What's the point in arguing, after all this time? But deep within me, the resentment that has never gone away rears its head and growls.

When I was younger, with my siblings, I was always the mediator, and I'd back down in arguments, preferring to keep the peace than to be right. But that all changed after I broke up with Victoria. I thought I'd gotten over what happened, but of course I haven't. The parting words of my ex, Emma, come back to haunt me. "You've got a persecution complex, Theo. You're so defensive all the time. It's exhausting."

She was right; I felt resentful if I thought she was accusing me of something I hadn't done, and I probably overreacted every time. That's Victoria's fault. She made me like that.

She's acting as if she's doing me a favor by forgiving me. But I don't need forgiving. I didn't do anything wrong. And I'm damned if I'm going to let her continue to make me feel as if I did.

I thought what happened between us was like an extinct volcano, but now I realize it was only dormant. It's beginning to smoke, and I can feel the first rumblings of an eruption.

We're going to have to talk about it, that's inevitable. But I'll hold my peace for now, until the moment's right.

Chapter Five

Victoria

I walk slowly along the beach, the water washing over my toes.

My stomach is churning with a mixture of acute hunger and conflicting emotions. It was obvious from the look on Theo's face that he won't admit he did anything wrong back then. He's still angry, still in denial, even after all this time. I want to go back to him and demand to know why he won't admit what he did was wrong, but I don't have the energy.

I get to the end of the sand and stop. I'm in a bit of a daze. My limbs are shaking, and I haven't been paying attention to what's around me.

In front of me is a line of palm trees, and the leaves of the final one stretch over the rocks. I lower onto a flattish one under the shade, too exhausted to do anything else. I know we need to look for food and water, but honestly I'm not sure where to start. I'm hardly an outdoor sort of girl. I've never enjoyed camping, and I've never been in the Scouts like Theo. My food has always come cleaned, chopped, cooked, and wrapped.

I think back to the resort in Fiji where I recorded my last daily yoga video, and give a short laugh. I'd called it Desert Island Yoga, thinking my fans would enjoy a visit to the South Pacific. But it was hardly a desert island in the truest sense of the word. I'd had a fridge filled with lemon tea and bottles of water, as much ice as I wanted, a beautiful pool, thick towels, a huge soft bed, and room service with a large menu of so many different dishes I never got to try them all.

Now look at me. I'd felt so relieved when we landed, and I'd felt solid ground beneath my feet. But now I just feel despondent and depressed. It doesn't matter that we've found land—I'm still going to die out here. So many things could go wrong. I could get injured—

what if I fall and break my leg? I could be stung by jellyfish or bitten by any number of insects. We might not be able to find food or water, or I'll get skin cancer and die a slow, painful death.

And why, oh why did I have to be marooned with Theo Prince?

Tears leak out of my eyes and run down my cheeks, and I'm too tired to wipe them away. It took me so long to get over him, but I eventually managed to get to the point where I didn't think about him every day. But seeing him has made it feel as if no time has elapsed at all. The hurt and bitterness is as fresh as it ever was.

It's only now, sitting here on this rock looking out to sea, that I finally admit to myself I've never gotten over him. What happened between us affected me deeply, and it's soured every relationship I've had since. My grief is a raw wound that hasn't closed over, and seeing him again is like someone poking that wound and making it bleed.

I put my face in my hands. I'm so tired. I wish it was all over.

"Victoria? Here." Theo pushes something into my hands. "Drink."

I open my eyes to discover a coconut with a hole in the top.

"It's lovely," he says. "I've had two already. Go on."

I raise it to my lips and tip it up, hoping some insect doesn't come crawling out, but cool sweet water fills my mouth, and I drink it down thirstily.

While I'm doing that, he takes another coconut and a small pointed rock, inserts the point into the end where it was joined to the tree, and twists it until a hole appears. Then he passes it to me. I tip it up and drink it, almost crying with relief.

He takes the first coconut and smashes it down hard on the rocks. After a couple of goes, it breaks open to reveal a kind of creamy-white cake.

"It looks like a brain," I mumble.

He laughs and breaks off a piece. "It's sprouted coconut. It's better roasted, but for now let's just get some carbs down us." He sits on the rock beside me, and we stuff big pieces of the coconut cake into our mouths and chew. I don't think I've ever tasted anything as magnificent.

He breaks open another, and we eat under the shade of the palm tree, listening to the waves lapping at the rocks, until the gnawing hunger has subsided. When he passes me another piece, I shake my head and flop back onto the rock. My limbs have stopped quivering, and the lightheadedness is passing.

"I don't feel so dizzy now," I tell him.

He stretches out beside me. "I guess that's the carbs. Well, there are plenty of coconuts, so we won't starve, although it's not exactly a varied diet. We'll explore in a while and see what else the island can offer."

I turn my head to look at him. "Theo… what are we going to do?"

He shades his eyes and looks at me. "About what?"

"About us."

We study each other quietly.

"I know we're not going to be able to make what happened go away," I tell him. "But I don't want to spend our time here feeling awful."

"I know what you mean."

"I want to talk about it," I say. "But how do we do that without getting angry at each other? One of us is going to have to change, and I don't know if either of us can do that."

What I mean is, I don't know if *he* can do that. Because I definitely can't. I will never, ever be able to forgive him. He's going to have to admit he did wrong. He wasn't able to do that before. And by the look on his face, I don't think he can do it now.

"We will talk about it," he says eventually. "But I suggest we wait a while, until we've made ourselves comfortable here. We've got a lot to do—explore the island, find food, water, shelter, start a fire… These things are too important to waste time arguing over minor stuff."

"Minor stuff?" Is that how he thinks of what happened?

"I meant in relation to our current situation, obviously."

I bite my lip. I know what he means, and he's right, so I nod my agreement. "Survival first."

"All right." He pushes himself up. "How are you feeling?"

"A bit better."

"Maybe we should pull the dinghy up the beach. We could sleep in it—it might stop insects crawling over us in the night."

"I like the sound of that."

So we get down from the rocks, go over to the life raft, and pull it to the top of the sand, where the waves can't reach it. After that, we decide our next step is to explore the island and find out what resources we have.

"You could do with some shoes, really," he says. "You don't want to cut your feet on stones or twigs."

"I was thinking about that. I saw a program once where a woman made shoes out of her bra."

His eyebrows rise. "Right."

"And now you're thinking about my boobs."

"I'm always thinking about your boobs. Get it off, then, and we'll see what we can do."

I remove the bra by unhooking it and then pulling the straps beneath the sleeves of my T-shirt, much to his fascination. He takes it from me, pointedly averting his gaze from my breasts.

"It's underwired," he says. "We should keep the wire in case we need it."

He picks up the stone he found earlier that has a point and works a tiny hole in the fabric until he's able to remove the two pieces of wire. Placing them to one side, he then rubs hard in the middle of the bra until it breaks apart.

"I wish I was a DD cup," I say, taking one of the B cups, which only covers about half of the sole of my foot.

"I'm not saying anything." He picks up the strap and manages to loop it around the top half of my foot to secure the cup there. "That's better than nothing."

We do the same with the other cup. It's hardly a shoe, but it might provide some protection.

"I could try weaving some leaves together later," I say. "I should be able to make all kinds of things like that."

"Great. Come on, then. Let's explore. I don't think it's going to take us long."

By the time we've circumnavigated the island, the sun is high in the sky. We're both exhausted and dispirited. The beach where we landed is the only sand we've found. Most of the island is rock covered with dense bush. We discovered no caves on the shoreline, and no running water. It's possible there is a cave higher up, but we're both too exhausted to climb.

We've just expended a huge amount of energy and for no real reward. The only thing we found that's even remotely positive are a couple of lemon trees, the fruit hanging heavy and ripe from the branches. We return to the rocks beneath the coconut trees, break open a couple more coconuts, and drink and eat while we gather our strength again.

"Well, that was a waste of time," I say.

"No it wasn't. It's important for us to explore the environment. Let's look at the positives."

"There are positives?"

"We landed in the best place on the island," he says. "We've got a little shade and coconuts, which means we're already better off than we were yesterday. Now we know this is the best place to be, we can work on the other things. We need to build a shelter. And we need to make a fire—for heat, for protection, to cook food, and to make a signal."

"What food?" I say sarcastically. "More coconut?"

His eyes meet mine, and I feel a touch of shame. I'm being spoiled and childish. I'm not normally like this. I think it's the lack of food and proper sleep, and, if I'm perfectly honest, I think the absence of my phone is affecting me more than I realized, which shocks me. Had I become so reliant on it that its disappearance can have a physical effect on me? The answer has to be yes. I've become an addict. My hand feels empty, and it's odd not to be able to look at the screen all the time. I feel jittery and weepy, and completely lost.

I'm absolutely furious to be in this position, and I want to punish someone for it. But much as I'd love to blame him, it's not Theo's fault, and I'm not going to improve the mood, or our chances of survival, by being petulant.

"I'm sorry," I say quietly. "Let's start with fire. I'm guessing we need dry wood?"

"Yes. We can try the fire-plow method—pretty much rubbing two sticks together. But it would be easier if we had some kind of lens."

"To direct the sun?"

He nods. "A glass bottle, or even a plastic bottle would do. Maybe we should start by collecting all the rubbish that's been washed up—we might even find something we could use as a knife. Let's walk along the beach and bring it all back over here."

"What are you expecting to find?" I ask as we get down from the rocks. "I've seen *Castaway*. Tom Hanks had lots of packages from his FedEx plane wash up on his island. I doubt we'll find a pair of ice skates. We'll probably find a couple of cigarette butts from a fishing ship and that'll be it."

"I've already had a walk up the beach," he says. "You're going to be very surprised. Things wash up from cruise ships, fishing trawlers, sunken containers, and from the nearby islands. It's quite shocking really."

Sometime later, as we stand in front of a huge pile of objects we've collected, I have to conclude he's absolutely right—it is shocking. We've found hundreds of items, all brought here by the tide.

There are seven empty glass bottles, and an amazing twenty-nine plastic ones ranging from small to large soda bottles, and one large container about two foot high. A couple of piles of knotted rope. Three ripped fishing nets. Two rubber ducks. A ball of tightly knotted red string. Five plastic toothbrushes. Four pieces of LEGO. A square of torn tarpaulin. A dirty torn bit of cloth screwed in a ball. A light bulb, still unbroken. A couple of balls. A baseball cap with a hole in the top. A denim jacket, very dirty and ripped in several places. A plastic box half-filled with butterfly hair clips. A Rubik's cube that doesn't work. A very dirty soft toy rabbit with half an ear missing. Half of a pair of dentures. A laundry basket with a Japanese label. A plastic comb with some of its teeth missing. And lots and lots of pieces of rusted metal or fragments of plastic from unidentifiable objects.

"Wow," I say. "I'm stunned."

"Told you." He bends and rifles through the objects. "Well the rope will come in handy. We can wash it and lay it out to dry. Same with the cloth items. We can use the tarpaulin for the shelter."

"The hair clips will pin stuff up," I add.

"Yes, and my tie. The bottles will be handy to catch rainwater and maybe even fish."

"What about making the fire?"

"Yeah, let's start with that."

He half fills one of the glass bottles with seawater while I collect an armful of dry wood and leaves. I bring it over to the area in front of the palm trees by the rocks, which seems to be the most likely place for our shelter, but far enough away so the bush shouldn't catch fire.

Theo makes a sort of cage of sticks over the smaller twigs and dry leaves. He sits to one side and positions the glass bottle so the sun is shining directly on it. Then we both wait.

My gaze drifts to his face while he concentrates on holding the bottle steady. He now has several days' growth of beard. When clean-shaven, he's model-handsome in a classic, almost beautiful way, and although he has bed hair, it's always because he's teased it that way with product. Now it's naturally messy, and his dark stubble has coarsened his fine features. His shirt is surprisingly clean but only bears two buttons. His trousers are covered with sand.

I quite like rough Theo. He's a man now, through and through.

He lifts his gaze to mine, catching me looking at him. "Don't laugh at my hair," he says.

"It's difficult not to. Especially when I look so perfect."

He laughs.

"I'm so glad I don't have a mirror," I add. I run a hand through my hair, which is damp and severely tangled. "I have no idea how I'm going to get these knots out. It might be easier to cut it."

"I've never seen you with short hair."

"I've never had it. In the movies, when characters are on the run, like in *The Bourne Identity*, the girl cuts her hair off and it looks as if a stylist has taken hours making it a neat bob. What's the betting when we do it, it looks as if someone's cut it with a knife and fork?"

"I'll use the comb we found," Theo says. "We'll detangle it. Don't cut it."

He used to love my hair, back in the day. He'd thread his hands through it while we lay in bed, and trail it over his body. He used to like me being on top, and the way it would fall around his face when I bent to kiss him.

I can see in his eyes he's thinking the same thing.

The smell of smoke fills my nostrils, and I look down to see a tiny flame leap into life. "Theo!"

He follows my gaze. "Whoa!" He bends and blows gently on it, the tinder flares, and the twigs catch fire. We add more dry wood, and soon a proper fire is blazing away.

"Man make fire!" He flexes his muscles. "Wow, I feel so incredibly masculine right now. I need to wrestle a bear or something."

He grins, and I smile back at our little triumph.

I push the memory of our lovemaking to the back of my mind. I'm not going to think about being on top of Theo Prince. Of how he'd hold my hips as he thrust up into me, or the expert way he'd grab me and toss me onto my back so he could take control.

The last thing I'm going to think about is how he'd kiss me for hours, until I had to beg him to take me.

I'm not going to dwell on the fact that the two of us are marooned on this tiny island, and might be stuck together for a significant amount of time. Just me and him. Alone. Wearing practically next to nothing.

I'm not going to think about it at all.

Chapter Six

Theo

It's tempting to pile every piece of driftwood we can find onto the fire to make it a roaring blaze, ready in case a plane flies overhead. But on the horizon, rain clouds are gathering, and I don't want to waste all the wood and find the fire is out within an hour. So we make sure it's leaping nicely, then turn our attention to making a shelter.

It takes several hours. We use the piece of tarpaulin we found on the beach, washing it first and then using the hair clips to pin it up between the palm trees so it forms a slanted roof. We then pull down some of the palm leaves and use the rope to keep them in place, until eventually we have a very loose kind of hut that'll give us a little shelter from the weather. Underneath it, the dinghy has pride of place, as it's going to serve as our bed for a while. The shelter won't be waterproof by any means, but it'll do for a start.

Victoria soaks the dirty piece of cloth in the sea and discovers it's a woolen poncho that will double very nicely as a blanket. She scrubs it on the rocks several times and does the same with the jacket, leaving them out in the sun to dry, then spends some time unknotting and washing the rope and red string. While she's doing that, I take a look in the rock pools. This is going to be our best bet for food as we didn't see any animals when we walked around the island.

One small fish is stranded in one of the pools, and that will have to do until I can make some traps. I construct a net by binding some sticks in a triangle and draping part of one of the fishing nets across them, then scoop the fish out of the rock pool. A flat rock sits not far from the shelter, and I clean the fish there—not my favorite job, but someone's got to do it—and take it across to the fire, where I put it on a stick and set it to cook, squeezing a little lemon over it to give it some flavor.

It is only then that something occurs to me. "Are you going to be all right eating this?"

Victoria is checking the dried jacket and blanket all over, presumably to make sure nothing is hiding inside. She looks over at me. "What are you talking about?"

"Aren't you a vegetarian? Are you going to be all right eating fish?"

She hesitates, then gives a sharp nod. "I might balk at eating meat, but I don't want to starve here, so it'll have to do."

It's starting to rain, so she picks up the blanket and the jacket and takes them into the shelter. We're going to have to try to protect some of the driftwood from the rain, or else it'll smoke when we burn it. The fire has a little protection from the circle of trees, but it won't last much longer in the rain. I leave the fish cooking over it, and prop up the big plastic container and some of the smaller bottles to catch rainwater. Then I join her, climbing in the dinghy under the roof.

We sit there and exchange a glance as rain filters in through the gaps and patters on the rubber raft.

"Perfect," she says. Then she sighs. "I don't think we've done too badly for our first day. Shame we didn't find a river for water."

"It's the one positive thing about it being the rainy season. We'll have to make do with collecting the rainwater, and if it does go dry, I'll try to make a solar still. I think I can remember how."

"I guess we have your grandfather to thank for most of this," she says.

"Yeah." I don't really want to talk about Granddad. The grief is still incredibly raw, building up like water behind a dam. I know it's going to burst at some point, but for now I want to try and keep it locked away. I'm afraid that if I give in to my emotion, the panic will leak out and I won't be able to plug the hole again. For Victoria's sake—and my own mental health—I want to try to stay in control.

"I think we should be really proud of ourselves," I say. "We've nearly got through the first day, and we haven't killed each other yet."

She gives a short laugh and throws me a wry look. "Don't think I haven't thought about it."

I bite my tongue. I'm not going to react to her barbed comments. Not yet.

"So what are our tasks for tomorrow?" she asks.

"I want to sort out some traps for fish and the rock pools. We need to think about a better signal fire, but it's going to be difficult if it's raining every day. We'll have to try to keep some wood as dry as we can, and then just rebuild the fire every day. Although we won't be able to light it if there isn't any sunshine."

"It's strange to be so guided by nature," she says. "Normally I pay very little attention to it, unless it's raining, which is always seen as a drag. But at the moment it's a good thing because we can catch the rainwater."

"You used to love going for walks and doing yoga outside. What happened?"

She looks away, out at the rain. "I grew up."

I study her profile. She's scooped her hair back off her face and tied it with a strand from the rope, but it's still horribly tangled. She looks fresh and very young without any makeup. I find it sad that she's become so jaded.

Her stomach rumbles loudly. "Sorry," she says, putting a hand on it.

"The fish should be done by now." I get up out of the dinghy. First I break open a couple more coconuts and pass them through to her. Then I check the fish, which is cooked, if a little dry, put it on a large leaf, and bring that in too, climbing back into the dinghy. She inspects the fish cautiously and tries a little bit. She swallows and meets my gaze, but she doesn't say anything. I know it must be tough for her as a vegetarian to eat something that's been alive, but unfortunately we don't have an option as the coconut isn't really enough to stave off our hunger. I just hope the fish won't upset her stomach too much.

We eat quietly, listening to the rain, and quench our thirst with the coconut water. When I'm done, I go back outside and collect the old plastic comb we found, rinse it in the sea, then climb back into the dingy.

"Turn around," I direct her. "I'll try to get some of the knots out of your hair."

"I can do that myself."

"You don't have a mirror. It'll be easier if I do it."

She doesn't reply, and to my surprise I see tears glistening on her lashes. She was never one of those women who cried at the drop of a hat when we were together, so I know she must be feeling under the weather and sorry for herself.

"Don't read too much into it," I say softly. "Come on, we're stuck here together and we just need to get through until we're rescued. We might as well help each other where we can."

She hesitates, then gives a little nod. I sit with my back against the edge of the raft, cross my legs, and gesture for her to scoot down. She lays with her head in my lap. I lift the mass of hair like a yellow fishing net, and I begin to work through the first knot, trying to untangle it.

I work in silence for a while. It's odd having no noise except the rain and the waves outside. I hadn't realized how much noise we have at home—traffic outside, the TV or music on, and of course the electrical hum of the heat pump or fans, computers, and all the other household devices we own.

I find the grooming strangely calming, rewarding even, gradually working my way through each section of her hair. It's going to take a while to get through it all, but we're in no hurry, and the light is starting to fade, so we can't do much more outside for now.

She sighs again, and it makes me think of what she said to me while we were at sea.

"Why did you tell me you were empty?" I ask. "You said you'd lost your connection with the divine, and you weren't sure you'd ever find it again. I asked if it was because of your ex, and you said you didn't want to talk about it. But I'd like to know. Can you tell me now?"

For a while she remains quiet, and we continue to listen to the rain pattering outside, while I work the comb through her hair.

Eventually, she says, "What do you know about my accident?"

"Only what I've read on the Internet. Your car crashed on the motorway. I know you had to be cut out. You were in hospital for a while. You obviously received that scratch on your cheek."

I've never had a car accident, but Lucas has, and I know it shook him up quite a bit. Obviously, it must have had an effect on her, too.

"Jack was driving," she says.

"Right."

"We were arguing when we crashed," she says.

My hands still for a moment, then continue combing. "What about?"

"We argued all the time. It was always about trust."

I stop combing again and close my eyes for a moment. What an idiot. I shouldn't have pushed her to explain.

"I was never able to trust him," she continued. "Every time we were apart, I worried about what he was up to. It ate into me like a sort of cancer. I used to demand to know where he was going, and who he was going with. He got more and more resentful. Now, I can see why, but at the time I thought it was because he was trying to hide something from me."

I try not to clamp down on my resentment. "So what actually happened in the car?"

"It wasn't like he was drunk. We didn't fight over the wheel or anything ridiculous like that. But we were arguing, and I suppose he must have lost concentration. He went to overtake and move into the outside lane, and there was a car behind us. He pulled out straight into its path, it hit us in the back, and we spun off the road. It was terrifying. We crashed straight into the barrier, and several cars piled into us."

"That must have been awful."

"It was. Luckily, I don't remember much about the aftermath. I hit my head on the window and blacked out. That's why they kept me in for a while, in case I had concussion. I was lucky though; I didn't break any limbs or anything. It could have been much worse."

"And you broke up after that?"

"Jack came to see me in the hospital. He'd broken his arm. He didn't even sit down. He stood there and apologized for not concentrating and causing the crash. Then he said, 'I think we're done,' and he walked away, and that was it. I haven't seen him since. He hasn't even rung me."

"Vic, that's awful."

"I'm not surprised. It was never going to work. I think I'm broken."

My arms are aching, and I lower them for a while. We sit in the gathering gloom, and I digest her words slowly, as if they were a huge meal.

"You think I'm to blame," I whisper. It's a statement, not a question.

"I know it began with my parents," she replies. "What happened between us just compounded it."

I look out at the fire. It's still burning, although there's a slight hiss every time a raindrop lands on the hot embers.

Victoria's father had an affair when she was fourteen years old. Her mother was so devastated by it, she took an overdose of pills and killed herself. Victoria has never gotten over it. She was still angry with her father when we met, and they hardly spoke. I can feel from the tenseness in her body that she's still angry with him now.

I continue combing her hair. "How is your dad?" I ask eventually.

"He's had a string of girlfriends over the years. He's with a woman called Gemma now, and they have a couple of young kids. I hardly see him. He says he's busy with work, but it's because he doesn't like seeing me either. I remind him of my mum too much." She looks outside.

"It's tough living with someone who has depression," I say carefully. "They often retreat into themselves, and it's possible he felt very lonely."

"That doesn't excuse what he did."

"No, I know."

She clears her throat. "Darkness falls so quickly in the islands, doesn't it? There's hardly any twilight."

"Yeah, it'll be dark soon." I know better than to push the matter. I work on a knot by her temple, slowing my hands as she winces when I pull. "So what happened with Jack… it affected your work? Your attitude toward your yoga?"

"It was already happening before that, but yes, it was the nail in the coffin if you like. It made me question everything. Since then I've not been able to motivate myself. I feel so miserable all the time. I can't meditate, and the yoga feels meaningless, not spiritual at all. The… company has become very materialistic, concentrating more and more on merchandise… against my wishes. I've been going through the motions for months. I know my fans have seen it, and I know I have to be careful or I'm going to lose everything I've spent so long building up. But I'm not sure what to do."

The final tangle is done, and now her hair lies in my lap like yellow wool, rich and soft. I don't want to let her go, though, so I continue to comb it slowly. She doesn't move either. I think she's enjoying the contact, although I know she'd never admit it.

Her statement that her company has become more materialistic against her wishes puzzles me. Is she talking about Beth?

"Maybe this will clear your head," I say. "Being on the island, I mean. Some peace and quiet for a few days, no phones or internet, nobody demanding anything from you."

"Maybe. But I don't know how I can fix this… sickness, I guess, in my soul. It's too deep. I don't think I can ever put it right. And if I can't, I'll never be able to have a successful relationship. Never be able to get married or have kids. And I want that so desperately, but it's out of my reach." She stops as her voice catches, then abruptly gets up, climbs out of the dinghy, and walks out of our shelter and down the beach.

I don't follow, because I'm guessing she needs some time to compose herself.

I don't know what to say to her, or how to make things right. What happened to her parents skewed her view of men, and what happened between us compounded it.

She thinks I cheated on her. She was convinced of it back then, and she's still convinced of it now. And because of that, she's obviously found it impossible to trust any guy since.

It's my fault she's not happy. That she's not married with kids right now. And yet there's nothing I could have done about it.

Because I didn't cheat on her.

I loved her. Still do, if I'm perfectly honest. That's not to say she hasn't hurt me. Or that I'll be able to forgive her easily for assuming I'd betray her.

But I feel as if I've been given a second chance to try to convince her I didn't do it.

The only question is, will she believe me?

Chapter Seven

Victoria

I stride across the beach and head into the bush. The trees gradually close around me, shrouding me in the noises and smells of night.

I stop, not wanting to go in too deep, but needing some time on my own. For a start, I need the toilet for the first time since we came to the island. My body kind of locked up for several days through terror, but finally it feels as if my digestive system has started working again, and my stomach is churning. I expect that's the fish as I feel nauseous too. I didn't want to sound like a child by refusing to eat when obviously we need to keep our calories up and I was really hungry, but it was a real struggle to swallow the fish, and now I'm sure it's disagreeing with me.

Frustrated and upset, I stomp around in the undergrowth until I find a spot that's slightly less uncomfortable than the rest, lower my underwear, and squat. It's too soon for the fish to have made its way through my system, surely, but my stomach turns itself inside out for a few minutes, and I hope Theo doesn't come looking for me as I groan and wait for it to be over.

When I'm finally done, I pick a large leaf and wipe myself, dreaming about using half a dozen sheets of ultra-thick toilet roll. I've just finished when I knock the plant beside me with my knee—and I recoil in horror as a huge spider the size of my hand scuttles across it before disappearing into the undergrowth.

I swear, loud and colorful, back away hurriedly, get to my feet, and go out of the bush. I turn away from the direction of the shelter and run down the beach a bit, and sink onto the sand, shaking and trembling.

Then I put my face in my hands and burst into tears.

I didn't scream when I saw the spider, and I don't want Theo to come running, so I try to cry quietly, but it's almost impossible. The tears pour down my face, and eventually I stop trying to hold them back and just sob and sob until my hands are wet, my nose is snotty, and my throat is sore.

Eventually I lower my hands, exhausted, and wrung out of all emotion. I sag onto the sand, too tired and dispirited to move.

I'd been wrapped up in my misery, but for the first time the sights and sounds of the night-time fill my senses. Insects chirrup and whirr in the bush behind me. The wash of the waves up the sand is soothing, and I realize it's stopped raining. I can smell the sea, and the rich, fertile scent of the trees in the undergrowth.

A slight breeze blows my hair around my face, and I run my fingers through it. Theo did well removing all the knots. It feels a bit sticky and dry. I'll wash it with some lemon juice tomorrow. It could do with a little conditioner. I wonder whether I can make some coconut oil?

Theo's hands combed my hair so tenderly... I drag my mind away from the memory.

The clouds part, and the moon shows through, a few days off full. A path of silvery light shines on the waves, like a line of silver tiles leading all the way up to her. A thousand stars glitter in the sky. It's breathtakingly beautiful.

I can't believe we're here, just the two of us, miles from civilization. No phone, no Internet, no fans, nobody pressing me to meet deadlines, no meetings, nothing I have to do by a certain time. I'm totally free. It's such a weird feeling. I've been bound by the clock for so long. It feels strange to have no idea what the time is. I'm guessing it's around eight p.m. as the sun has set.

If it had still been raining, the beach would be completely dark, but in the moonlight I watch Theo exit our shelter and walk slowly along the beach towards me. I don't move, though, composing myself before he arrives.

When I was telling him about Jack and the accident, it took all my self-restraint not to throw accusations at Theo, and to put all the blame on him. Of course, it's not all his fault, I know that. But what happened between us definitely had an impact on my future relationships.

It's strange, but after we broke up, he kind of stayed frozen in my mind. Whenever I thought about him, I pictured him as he was back then, even though I've seen photos of him since. I imagined if we met up again that our feelings towards each other would have stayed the same as they were, caught in time like a fly in amber.

In some ways they have, but it's only now as I watch him approach that I realize how much time has passed. Seven years is a long time to keep the more vitriolic emotions fresh—hate, resentment, and anger. They're like the lava that spills from a volcano when it erupts. At the time of our breakup, the pyroclastic flow of my fury swept right over me and burnt me to a crisp. But over time, the lava hardened, and even though deep down inside me resentment still bubbles away, a lot of the more painful emotions have cooled.

In my head, I'd made him into some kind of ogre, this evil man who had set out to hurt me, who'd taken away my innocence, and who'd corrupted and tarnished me for every man who came after.

Now, though, I understand he was just a guy who made a mistake, and although that doesn't excuse what happened, I can see it as just a human failing. Did he deserve the amount of anger and hatred I poured onto him? Maybe he did back then, but he doesn't deserve it now.

He comes up to me and drops to his haunches. "Hey. How are you doing?"

"I saw a huntsman spider," I tell him, rubbing my nose. "Big as my hand. Frightened the shit out of me."

He chuckles and looks over his shoulder into the bush. "What happened to it?"

"It ran off into the undergrowth. I didn't hurt it. It was here before we were. Mind you, if it comes into the shelter, I'll crush it to a pulp."

"Fair enough." He turns and looks out to sea, and I study his profile, the lean angles of his body. He's taken off his shoes and socks, and his bare feet have made silver prints in the sand. Only Theo could be stranded on a desert island in a suit. He looks smart, rugged, and rough and ready, all rolled into one. He's still so incredibly handsome. He takes my breath away.

"Are you coming back to the shelter?" he asks.

I look out to sea. "Actually, I'm enjoying just sitting here now the rain's stopped."

I half expect him to turn and head back, but he lowers to the sand beside me. "I'm sorry if I upset you back there."

I shake my head. "It wasn't you. The tension of the last few days suddenly overwhelmed me." I sigh. "Plus, and I know this is a bit TMI but I'm hardly going to be able to hide it from you, I think I'm a bit emotional because my period is due."

"Ah."

"I have the jab—the contraceptive injection. I had one a month ago so it should last another couple of months. My periods are light now, but I still get a bit emotional beforehand. Sorry."

"Don't apologize, I think we've done well in getting as far as we have without turning into gibbering wrecks."

I chuckle. "I suppose we have to count each day we get through as a success."

"Definitely."

I look at the planes of his face, where the moon highlights his cheekbones and the straight line of his nose. His cheeks and chin are dark; soon he'll have a beard, not just stubble.

I wonder how many girlfriends he's had since we broke up? I've seen him on social media several times, usually with a different girl on his arm, although I know he went out with Emma Fanshaw for quite a while. There were photos of them in all the women's magazines. She was tall and dark-haired, which surprised me as I thought he preferred blondes.

"How many times have you been in love over the last seven years?" I ask him on impulse, before I can think better of it.

He gives me an amused look. "In love?"

"Come on, you can tell me."

"I dunno. I've liked all the girls I've dated. I'm not sure at what point like officially turns into love."

"Well, that's not really what I'm talking about. Loving someone and being in love with them are two different things."

He gives me a blank look.

"Come on, Theo. Being in love with someone is when you can't stop thinking about them, when they're on your mind all the time. When your heart races as they walk in the room. Loving them is something that happens over time—it comes with comfort and security. You must know what I mean."

"Sort of."

"You must have loved Emma. You were with her, what, two years?"

"About that."

"Where did you meet her?"

"Through Kora," he says, naming his twin sister. "She fixed us up on a blind date. I'm not normally into that sort of thing, but I'd been single for a while, and she was sure we'd get on. We went out for dinner, hit it off straight away, and started dating. It was pretty smooth sailing."

"Did she move in with you?"

"No, she stayed over a lot, but we never took that step."

"So, were you in love with her?" I'm not sure why I'm pushing him. Maybe I need to hear him say that he's loved other women, to erase the feeling that somehow we were meant to be together, meant to be soulmates, and blew it.

He picks up a stick and draws spirals in the sand in front of him. I watch him attempt to form his thoughts. Eventually, he says, "Honestly? You're the only woman I've ever been in love with. And the only woman I've ever loved. In both senses of the word."

I stare at him. "You must have loved Emma."

He thrusts the stick into the sand. "Not the same way I loved you."

I don't know what to say to that. I can't yell at him and ask what the hell he thinks he's saying because I'm the one who asked the question. I can't get angry because I don't like the answer.

But I don't want to know that I'm the only woman he's ever been in love with. Because it implies I'm as much to blame for his present condition as he is for mine. And that's not fair. I only reacted to what he did, I didn't cause the end of our relationship.

We sit side-by-side, listen to the sound of the waves on the sand. I don't want to argue with him. I'm too tired, and I don't want to ruin the rest of our time on this island. It could be some time before we're rescued, and it's going to be impossible to get through if we're both angry with each other all the time.

Equally, it seems ridiculous to live on either side of the island and not see each other. Human beings need company and support, and it makes sense to help each other out while we stay here.

We need to get by as best as we can, and the only way to do that is not to poke the sore, bleeding wound of our relationship with a stick.

"It's my fault for starting it," I murmur, "but we should stop talking about this."

He sighs. "Yeah, you're probably right."

"Maybe we should put a moratorium on anything to do with feelings and past relationships."

He tosses the stick away. "I know what you're saying. Oddly, though, I feel better for talking about it, even if it makes us uncomfortable. It's like we're excavating the past, peeling back the layers, until we get to what lies underneath it all."

"I'm not sure I want to go back that far."

"We will," he says with certainty. "But not tonight. Come on, let's go back to the shelter. It'll get cold soon, and we should get some rest so we're ready for first light tomorrow."

I let him pull me to my feet, and we walk back slowly across the sand to our tiny house. Calling it a house is a bit of a stretch, but it's nice to think of it that way. We duck under the tarpaulin and get into the dinghy. The poncho I washed earlier today is stiff and small, but it's better than nothing, and we sit side-by-side and pull it over our knees. Theo hands me half a coconut, and I have a drink and then nibble the coconut cake inside, listening to the sound of the waves.

"So what do we have planned for tomorrow?" I ask.

"We've got quite a lot of things to do. We can carry on improving the shelter. Try making it a little more waterproof. You said you might have a go at weaving some leaves, and that'll help us shore up the walls and the roof. I'll make us a new fire, as long as it doesn't rain too hard during the night. We'll make it nice and big, so we can signal if anybody flies overhead. I'm going to set some fish traps, although I'm a bit worried about you eating them. You're not used to that kind of protein, and it might make you ill."

"I do feel a bit queasy." I decide not to tell him about my diarrhea.

"We'll also have a look for some vegetables in the bush, see if we can find anything. I want to make a knife too, maybe by using some clamshells or some glass from one of the bottles, set into the handle. That will make things a lot easier."

I feel my arm sting, and I slap my hand on it, knowing I've been bitten by a mosquito. "Is there anything we can do about these?" I ask, annoyed. "We're going to get eaten alive."

"Unfortunately not. We'll have to try to do our best not to scratch too much—we don't want to get infected."

I rest my head on the back of the raft. "Do you really think we'll be discovered?"

"Absolutely. Like I said, Dad won't stop until he finds us, and there aren't that many islands."

"I thought you said there were hundreds."

"Well, yeah, but what I mean is it's not an indefinite number. He'll fly around them all once, and then again, and then again, until he finds us."

I nod, but deep down I wonder whether he's being a bit fanciful. Surely, there comes a time when you have to give up looking for someone. I wonder whether any of the other rafts made it to land? And I wonder how far away we are from them. Maybe we got pushed in a different direction by the weather, and they're looking in the wrong place. At some point, if we're not found, they'll assume we drowned.

But I don't say this to Theo, who is obviously hanging on to the hope that his father is going to keep looking. I have to remind myself too that I'm not a nobody, I'm famous in my own way. Beth will be organizing something, I'm sure.

"I keep thinking of Lucy," I whisper. "I can't believe she's dead."

"I know. It's awful." He lifts up his arm and, without thinking, I lean against him. I'm shaking a little, and he rubs my arm and kisses the top of my head.

"We are going to make it," he says firmly. "We're young, fit, and resourceful, and we both have people who are going to be looking for us. We're going to get out of this, Vic. It won't be long before you're back to doing your yoga, putting your videos up, and telling all your fans about your adventures. Imagine what publicity you're going to get."

I rest my hand on his chest, feeling the thud of his heart beneath his ribs. At the moment, I can't imagine ever sleeping in a warm bed or eating lovely food again.

I'm probably going to die here.

I concentrate on my breathing while I wait for the panic to die down. It's probably not going to happen. I have to be positive. But part of me feels it's important to come to terms with the notion that we might not be rescued.

If I don't fall ill and die from disease or an accident, I could have forty or fifty years stuck here.

With Theo.

It's a strange thought. And I surprise myself by realizing that maybe, just maybe, it wouldn't be the worst thing in the world.

Chapter Eight

Theo

It rains in the night, a passing shower that wakes me, pattering on the tarpaulin roof. I lie awake for what must be an hour or so, finding it oddly comforting. Victoria is asleep, warm and soft next to me. Something rustles in the undergrowth behind us, bigger than an insect, but it doesn't come into our shelter. A lizard, maybe. I think I see a dark shape swooping across the moon at one point—perhaps a fruit bat, or maybe an owl.

The smell of the sea washes over me, along with the faint scent of Victoria's perfume that still lingers on her clothes—something deep and musky, not fruity or flowery and therefore different from the natural smells of the island. It stirs my senses, and I look down at her, just able to see the curve of her pale neck in the moonlight, and her beautiful blonde hair spread out across my arm, which she's using as a pillow.

I'm still in shock from what I admitted to her earlier. What a dumb thing to do. I feel as if I've cracked open my ribs and revealed my soft, squidgy heart to her. I can't imagine she'll handle it gently. It's more likely she'll reach in, take it in her hand, and squeeze until it oozes out between her fingers. It's what she did before, after all.

But it's done, and I surprise myself by feeling a lift in my spirits. No secrets, now. Nothing to hide from her. It's all out in the open.

I finally doze off, conscious of the touch of her lips and the whisper of her breath on my skin.

When I awake, it's light, and Victoria has gone. I sit up and peer out of the shelter. The tide is in, and she's sitting on the strip of sand that remains, a pile of palm fronds in front of her, in the process of weaving them. She's wound her hair high on her head in a loose bun, and fixed it in place using a couple of the hair clips we found.

She's also completely naked.

Holy moly.

She's presumably washed her clothes, because they're lying beside her, drying in the early sun.

I stare, transfixed. Her skin glows in the sunrise, a beautiful warm peach. Her hair is a dazzling natural blonde.

Her breasts are still firm and high, the nipples a light pinky-brown.

I have a hard on in seconds. Like, literally, seconds. Wow, that's the fastest it's happened since I was about sixteen.

I can't move. I'm transfixed by the sheer beauty of the moment—the natural scene of the gorgeous woman working quietly against the backdrop of the white sand, the lush green bush behind her, and beyond that the sky turned the color of coral by the sunrise.

For a moment I can't move, aware of the perfection of this snapshot in time. Suddenly I long for my phone. I'd love to share it with everyone who can't be here. For our generation, an event doesn't count unless you can show evidence you were there, and once time moves on I'll have no proof it ever happened.

But I have no phone, just my eyes to capture the scene, and so I drink in the smells and colors and the taste of salt on my tongue as I try to imprint it on my mind.

Then I realize I'm spying on her like a pervert, and I feel a stab of guilt and shame. I turn away and cough loudly as if I've just woken up, and rustle around in the shelter as I lever myself out of the dinghy.

By the time I exit, she's pulled on her clothes and is smiling as her fingers slide the leaves through one another.

"Morning," she says.

"Morning." I stretch and yawn, then suddenly remember the erection that hasn't quite disappeared yet. I drop my arms hastily, but it's too late; her eyes have widened and her lips are curving up.

"Interesting dream?" she asks, then gives a girlish giggle.

"I was thinking about apple pie and custard," I reply, heading for the bush.

"Fair enough." But her laughter follows me into the trees.

I smile as I relieve myself, checking to make sure the huntsman spider from last night isn't watching, then return to the sand. I check the plastic container we left out last night and am pleased to find it half full, as well as most of the other plastic bottles I pushed into the sand.

Victoria has left a coconut shell in front of it so she's obviously had a drink. I scoop up some of the water and quench my thirst.

"I've made us a wash box each," she says, indicating two small baskets she's woven. "Lemon leaves for washing, and mint leaves for chewing instead of toothpaste. I've really given the toothbrushes a good soak and a scrub, so they're all clean. I'm going to try to make some coconut oil later for our hair."

"Great idea, thanks." I pick one of the baskets and take it down to the water's edge, and decide a swim would be nice to wake myself up properly. I take off my shirt, hesitate, then shrug and strip off the rest of my clothes.

"Whoa," she says.

"You'll have to get used to this. I'm not wearing a suit the whole time we're here." I wade into the water.

"I'll weave you a pair of trunks," she calls out.

Laughing, I dive into the ocean. It's cool but not cold, and I swim along the beach rather than out too deep, not wanting to discover any jellyfish or sea snakes.

I do a dozen lengths up and down, using long, slow strokes, enjoying stretching my muscles and the feel of the water sliding across my skin. When my body feels nicely loose, I stop and retrieve the lemon leaves and scrub them over my skin, hoping it's enough to clean away any sweat and unpleasant smells.

Victoria continues to do her weaving, casting a glance at me every now and then. She looks more peaceful than she did last night, when she'd obviously been crying. Being practical helps, I think, and keeping busy. Well, it's not like we don't have anything to do. I'm aware it's the rainy season, and I'm sure we'll be hit by thunderstorms at some point, and possibly even a cyclone, so we'll need to explore the island again and find the best place to build a more permanent shelter.

But for now I think it's important to make ourselves as comfortable as possible, and that means food and fire. I wade back to the sand, smiling as Victoria dips her head to concentrate on her weaving, and pull on my boxers. I leave the rest of my clothes off until the sun is higher in the sky and there's a danger of burning.

Next to her on the sand sits a small object. I laugh as I realize she's washed the little toy rabbit. It's come up quite nicely, a light brown color with a black nose and beady eyes.

"Meet Watson," she says.

I grin, remembering Tom Hanks's Wilson from the movie. "Is he going to stop us from going mad?"

"Oh, I think we're both past that point, don't you?"

I chuckle and turn to the fire. "Breakfast time."

"Coconut," she says. "Woo hoo!"

I pick up a couple of coconuts make a hole in the top with a pointed stone. Then I take one over to her. As we drink, I inspect her weaving. She's made a rectangle two feet by three.

"I thought I'd make lots of these for now," she says, "and we can use them for the shelter, or baskets to carry things, or to eat on, whatever."

"Good idea. I'm going to make a new fire, then set some fish traps."

"Okay."

I use the glass bottle filled with water to light a fire, still amazed it works so well, then gather lots of dry driftwood and pile it on until it's roaring nicely. I bank it up with some bigger branches from the bush, hoping it's visible to any planes that might be circling overhead.

Then I spend an hour or so cutting the bottom off about half the plastic bottles, hunting for worms for bait, and placing stones in the bottom to weigh them down. I sit them in the bottom of the rocks and hope the fish that dash away when I come near will be attracted by the worms and then become trapped when the tide recedes. If that doesn't work, I'll have to resort to spear fishing. I have a feeling I'm going to be very hungry if that happens.

My next task is to fashion a knife. I could use a glass bottle, but I'm worried about cutting myself and getting infected, so that'll have to be a last resort. I collect a heap of clam shells and spend a frustrating amount of time binding them to a sturdy stick, but it works, and eventually I have a fairly solid blade that'll come in handy for cutting down leaves and maybe even chopping wood.

By this time the sun is high in the sky, and it's getting hot. I pull my shirt back on, although I leave my trousers off, and glance over at Victoria. She retreated into the shade of the trees next to the shelter a while ago, and she now has a dozen or so woven panels sitting next to her. I can see she's made one into a basket with a handle. She's rolled another up and tied it with rope that she separated into strands. She's currently doing her best to stuff it with grass, possibly to make a pillow. That'll be nice for tonight.

Man, it's hot. Longing for some sunglasses, I shade my eyes and look up at the sky, checking for rainclouds, but it's a pure, bright blue with just a streak of cirrus clouds high above us.

I blink and squint. What's that in the distance? A bird?

No, it's flying too straight and even.

"Victoria!" I yell, and I run to the middle of the beach. "It's a plane!"

She drops her weaving and dashes out to stand beside me. The two of us jump up and down and wave our arms, screaming at the top of our lungs, even though I know a pilot is never going to hear us. My heart races, and I will the plane with every ounce of my being to turn in the sky and head our way.

But it doesn't. It continues on its path, heading away from our island, far, far away. Too far to see us, I'm sure. I lower my arms, my chest heaving.

"Did it see us?" Victoria's face is full of hope.

"I don't think so."

She presses her fingers to her lips. "Have we missed our chance?"

"I left it too late to light the fire," I say bitterly. "I should have kept it going. We'll have to take shifts sleeping and make sure it lasts the night."

Her eyes fill with tears, and then suddenly she's crying, her face in her hands.

"It's all right," I say desperately, putting my arms around her. "They'll be back."

"You don't know that."

"I do. We'd have heard if they'd have flown overhead. Dad will divide the area into segments, and he'll make passes over each one methodically, one at a time, until he's done them all, and then he'll start again."

She's rigid in my arms as she fights for control. I rub her back and rest my lips on the top of her head, wishing I could make it better for her.

"Why don't I see if I've caught any fish?" I ask, conscious she must be hungry, because I'm ravenous.

She nods, turns away, and walks into the bush.

I sigh, wondering whether to go after her, but she might be having a pee, so I leave her to it and go over to the rock pools.

I'm thrilled to see two smallish fish in there, and the tide hasn't quite gone out yet. Using my net, I scoop them out, use my new knife to gut them, then put them on sticks and set them over the fire. Victoria has returned by this point, and she sits back beside the shelter and picks up her weaving. This time she looks less bright, though, understandably despondent.

When the fish is done, I cut it into pieces and bring it over to her with another opened coconut. She studies the fish.

"I've got an upset stomach," she says in a low voice.

I sit beside her, worried at the news. Diarrhea is nothing to laugh at when you don't have the minerals to replace those you're losing. "I'm sorry. But you have to eat, and make sure you keep drinking. We've plenty of rainwater at the moment."

She takes a piece of the fish and chews it slowly.

"You're doing well with the weaving," I say, trying to cheer her up.

"I've made you a pillow," she says, showing me.

"For me?" I'm touched she's made one for me first. "It's amazing, that's going to be so much more comfortable."

She gives a shadow of a smile, then shifts on the sand, obviously uncomfortable. Suddenly it clicks what might be the matter. "Has your period started?" I ask gently.

Her cheeks flush. "Yes. It's okay, luckily it's not too bad, it's fairly light. I cut a couple of strips off the bottom of my leggings, and I'll use those as pads."

"How are you feeling? Does your tummy hurt?"

"I'm all right," she says. But I remember she used to get a headache as well as the usual ache in her abdomen.

"Why don't you have a lie down for a while?" I suggest. "Stay out of the sun here and rest. You're going to be short on energy as you're not eating much, and you're probably still dehydrated. I'm going to have a little explore and see if I can find something else for you to eat."

"Okay," she whispers. "Thank you."

I go out and scoop some rainwater into one of the plastic bottles, squirt a little lemon juice in it, then bring it back to her. "Keep sipping water."

"Okay."

I hesitate. "Are you sure you're all right?"

Moisture glimmers on her lashes, but she nods.

"I won't be long," I tell her.

She nods and turns over, curling up away from me. I smile as I notice Watson the rabbit sitting next to her.

I pull on my trousers, socks, and shoes, collect my knife, and walk away. I don't think she's seriously ill, just feeling a bit sorry for herself, which is perfectly understandable. But I do need to see if I can find her something else to eat. She's been a vegetarian since she was sixteen, and her stomach isn't used to processing animal protein. The fish is probably better for her than a large steak would be, but it will still take some getting used to.

Mmm, steak. I sigh as I walk the length of the beach. A thick, medium-rare steak with a blue cheese sauce, chunky fries, and onion rings. And chocolate pudding with ice cream to finish.

Fantasizing about food gets me to the end of the sand, and I enter the trees that cluster together to form the dense bush that occupies most of the island. I'm not sure I have the energy to climb to the top of the peak in the middle, but I will take more time on the western side of the hill, as this was where the gulls were circling yesterday, and I might be lucky and find some eggs.

I don't like leaving Victoria alone, but I'm sure she'll probably doze off, and maybe she'll feel better when she wakes.

As I trample through the lush undergrowth, I think about the plane in the distance, and for the first time I contemplate the fact that it might be some time before we're found. I could end up living here, on this tiny island, with Victoria, for months or even years.

I think of her sitting naked on the sand. We're two young, healthy, sexually active people who are going to find it difficult to be celibate for an extended length of time. I wouldn't be a normal male if I didn't wonder if it was possible for our relationship to turn physical eventually. I know we'd need to resolve our differences first, and to find a sustainable source of food so we remain fit and healthy. But if we did...

Victoria said her injection would last another couple of months. I still have the three condoms in my wallet, but firstly, I imagine I'll end up using them to keep something watertight, and secondly, three wouldn't last very long if our sex life ended up being anything like it was before. My lips curve up for a second. Then my smile fades at the thought that she could get pregnant.

Women have been giving birth without modern medicine for hundreds of thousands of years. But even so, the thought of her having to bring a child into the world here, with only me to deliver it, is pretty horrific. What if the baby came early, or there was a problem with the birth? I don't know if I could live with myself if I got her pregnant and the baby died. Or she died. Oh God.

I shake my head fiercely and push some branches aside as I start to climb the main hill to the center of the island. There's absolutely no point in thinking about that kind of thing. At the moment, Victoria still bears huge resentment toward me, and she's made it very clear I'm not to make any advances on her. I couldn't convince her I was innocent when we were dating, and she's had seven years working with Beth since then, which is only going to have cemented their relationship. It's a big obstacle, and until we can overcome it, the only relationship I'm going to have here is with my right hand.

A strange noise makes me stop. That sounds like… I push aside a large branch and inhale sharply. Now that I didn't expect!

Chapter Nine

Victoria

When at last I open my eyes, the colors of the island have changed. I'm beginning to get used to them. In the morning, the sky is the color of coral and gold. As the day wears on, it turns light blue, then a very deep blue, the shade of Theo's eyes. Later, it takes on an orangey hue, and as the sun sets it becomes a huge bruise, with purples and yellows and even greens.

Now, it's brushed with orange and the sun is low over the horizon, so I know I've been asleep for several hours. I feel stiff from lying in the same position, and the left side of my body is covered in sand. I brush it off and push myself up. Only then do I realize what woke me. The smell of something cooking.

I turn and look at the fire. Theo has put fresh wood on it, and he's also heaped a whole lot of dry wood to one side under the cover of some of the palms, which might help to keep it dry.

He's sitting by the side of the fire, poking at something in the embers. I rise and walk toward him. He's taken a piece of the metal we discovered on the beach yesterday, cleaned it, and bent up the edges to form a rudimentary frying pan. In the middle of the pan, he's making scrambled eggs.

"Eggs!" I say, delighted.

"I found chickens!" He grins, looking so incredibly handsome and happy that it lifts my heart.

"Chickens?"

"Someone must have brought them to the island in the past and they've run wild. These eggs were still warm, so they've only been laid today. Don't they smell amazing?"

I drop to my knees by him and throw my arms around his neck. He immediately puts one arm around me and hugs me. "Aw," he says. "How are you feeling? You've been asleep for ages."

"Better, thank you. And yes, they do smell good." Over his shoulder, I also see some small objects in the embers. "What are they?"

"Taro, I think."

It's a starchy vegetable I had while I was in Fiji. "Oh my God, Theo!"

"I found some not far from the chickens. It looks like there are quite a few plants there. Hopefully it'll make you feel better to get some good food inside you."

"It will, I'm sure. Thank you."

"You're welcome." He returns to stirring the eggs. "I've got something else to show you, but we'll eat first. What shall we use for plates?"

"I'll grab some big leaves, shall I?"

"Just make sure there are no huntsman spiders underneath!"

I laugh. I'm willing to risk seeing another spider to have some scrambled eggs.

I return to the shelter and collect another of the sanitary pads I made earlier, from a wide strip of my leggings folded over and stuffed with grass. I go into the bush and replace it, then quickly take the old one behind our hut and down to the sea where I wash the cloth through, leaving it to dry on the rock. I'm pleased with myself for inventing something that worked, and I'm sure he feels the same.

I've taken so much for granted all my life. I'm so privileged, and I assumed I would be useless in an environment like this, without all the mod cons, but we've made fire, built a shelter, found food, and survived several nights. I don't think we're doing too badly at all.

I do acknowledge it would have been a lot harder without Theo. I can't imagine how I would have felt if I'd been in the raft alone. Living here on my own, having to forage for food and make fire myself. I know the survival instinct is strong, but I'm honestly not sure I would have made it. I think I might have thrown myself overboard within the first few hours.

But Theo is here, and we're doing okay, so I'm not going to think about it now. Instead, I go back to the trees, find two large roundish leaves, and bring them back to him.

"It's all ready," he says. He uses his new shell knife to drag the taros from the fire, and puts a couple on each plate. Then he cuts them down the middle. Steam spirals out, and he mashes them up a little with the tip of the knife. Finally he tips the cooked egg into the middle, so it almost looks like a baked potato.

"No butter," he says, disappointed. "Tomorrow I'm going to look for a cow."

I giggle, and he grins and hands me one of the plates. Together we sit on the sand and eat with our fingers, trying not to burn them on the hot food.

The egg has small pieces of what looks like a herb in it. "Seaweed," he says at my quizzical look. "Most of what you find in rock pools is edible. I tested it first, don't worry."

"I'm not—it looks amazing."

We don't speak again until we're finished, and we both mop up the remains with our fingers. My stomach rumbles contentedly, and I fall back with a sigh. "That's the most delicious thing I've ever eaten."

"I concur. It was amazing, if I say so myself."

"I'm going to call you chef from now on," I tell him, and he chuckles.

"I'll take that."

"I think you've saved my life, Theo, several times over now. I don't know if I can ever repay you."

"I'm sure I'll think of something."

I roll my head to look at him. His eyes sparkle.

"Cheeky," I say.

He sighs and looks up at the sky. "We've probably only had a couple of hundred calories, but I feel full up. Maybe we'll end up getting fat living here. They'll come and rescue us and find us the size of two beach balls."

That makes me laugh. "Seriously, though, I do appreciate everything you've done."

It's hard to balance his good-natured generosity against the way he treated me before. But then twenty-three to thirty is a big difference. Maybe he's just grown up.

"If you like this," he says, "you're going to love my next treat."

"Ooh."

"Come on." He gets up and holds out a hand, then pulls me to my feet. "Follow me."

He leads me past the shelter to the group of trees behind. We go through them, but not into the undergrowth; instead he takes me forward, to the other side where the bush meets the outcrop of rocks. The ground rises here, the palm trees growing at strange angles out of the rocky ground.

One of the fishing nets hangs from the trees, and he's threaded it through with trailing vines and flowers. It's so pretty!

"Ready?" He looks hesitant and excited at the same time. I nod, and he pulls back his makeshift curtain and gestures for me to go through.

I walk into a small area of sand about six feet square. Palm trees surround it on three sides, and he's interlaced their leaves and plaited them overhead so they form a kind of bower, and will give shade from the sun when it's at its highest. He's also collected hundreds of shells, and he's obviously used his knife to make small holes in the top, following which he's strung them from long strands of rope. They jangle in the sea breeze, and they flash in the sunlight, all sorts of beautiful colors—blues, purples, oranges, and vivid reds.

At the center on the ground is a large flat stone on the sand facing out to sea. He's covered it with dry grasses and one of my woven mats.

"I thought we could call it the Haven," he says. "The stone is where you meditate, and you can do your yoga on the sand, facing the sea and the rising sun."

I stare at him, so incredibly touched I'm speechless.

"I thought it might help you stop feeling empty," he explains, looking a bit embarrassed. "If you don't like, you don't have to use it…"

When I was about fourteen years old, just a few months before she found out about my father's affair and took her own life, my mother gave me a talk about boys. She explained that they relied on signals to know whether it was appropriate for them to touch us and to understand how far they could go. She told me it was important not to lead them on, and it was unfair to let them think I was interested in sleeping with them, only to refuse at the last moment. I've always remembered that lesson, and I've never shown a man interest if I wasn't willing to follow through and let that relationship develop.

I don't want to sleep with Theo. Well, that's not strictly true because he's gorgeous, and I haven't had sex in a while, and my memories of how good he was in bed are still incredibly vivid. But I know I mustn't sleep with Theo. I can't, because if I do, I'm going to fall for him again, and I'll open myself to being hurt for a second time.

He might have grown up, and he might have changed. But clichés are clichés for a reason, and they say a leopard can't change his spots. If he believed seven years ago it was okay to cheat on his girlfriend, it's unlikely he feels differently now.

So I'm not going to sleep with him. And I don't want to let him think that's a possibility.

But…

It's a gorgeous afternoon, and he's just been absolutely delightful to me. He took the time to find food I would like, and he made this wonderful nook for me. He cares about me, and therefore it's without regret or intention or anything but instinct that I go up to him, take his face in my hands, and kiss him.

He inhales sharply, and I move back an inch to look at him, wondering if he's going to be angry at my mixed signals, if he's going to say *What the hell do you think you're doing?*

He doesn't. Instead, his hand comes up to the back of my neck and his warm palm covers my nape, and he holds me there as he presses his lips to mine.

It's possibly the most beautiful kiss I've ever had, with the hot sun coming through the palm fronds to lie over us in stripes of gold, the glistening blue ocean applauding us on the rocks, seagulls calling overhead, and the soft sand between my toes. Theo's lips are warm and firm, and I have no hesitation in parting mine and receiving the gentle sweep of his tongue.

I slide my arms around his neck and press up against him, and the kiss warms and blossoms into a long, lazy embrace. The sea breeze whispers across my skin, and my nipples tighten where they're brushing against his chest, so I know he must be able to feel them.

His bristles prickle my face, but I like the feeling. I sink my hands into the short hair on the back of his head and surround myself with the feel, taste, and smell of him, making the most of the perfect moment.

It's only when I draw back that I feel the first twinge of guilt. He's quite a bit taller than me without my heels, and I look up at him, pressing my fingers to my lips.

"Theo…"

"I know," he says.

We study each other in the dappled sunshine.

I try again. "It doesn't mean—"

"I know," he says again.

Still, I feel I have to explain. "I shouldn't have kissed you."

He shrugs. He doesn't look annoyed. "It's a gorgeous afternoon," he says. "It seemed fitting."

I hesitate. "I wanted to say thank you for doing all this for me," I say softly. "And Theo... you know how I feel about you. I always have, and always will."

He looks down at the sand and curls his toes into it.

"But you know we can never... you know... again."

He lifts his gaze to me. Wow, his eyes are so blue, it's as if they're discs cut out of the sky.

I wait for him to say 'I know' again.

But he doesn't. He studies me for a long moment, and although he's not smiling, I'm sure there's amusement in his eyes.

Then he steps around me and pulls the curtain to one side. "I'll leave you to get acquainted with the Haven." And he walks out and lets the curtain drop.

I stare after him, then sink down onto the cushion he made for me on the flat stone. The ground here is a little higher than the rocks in front, and I have an awesome view of the shallow water and then the deeper ocean beyond.

I press my fingers to my lips again. They're still tingling from his kiss.

I close my eyes. That was such a stupid thing for me to do. I've opened the door to the possibility of there being something physical between us, which absolutely mustn't happen.

But it's impossible for me to regret it.

I lower my hand to my lap and let the ocean breeze sweep its warm fingers across my face.

I think of Lucy, of her fun teasing, and the way she batted her eyelashes when I introduced her to Theo. She'll never kiss a man again. Never make love. Never have children. A lump forms in my throat, but I don't fight the emotion—I let it sweep over me and bear me away on the wave.

I cry a little for her, and for the other passengers who died on the plane. For the children who'll never grow up. The parents who must have felt so helpless when they couldn't save them.

I'm sure survivor's guilt is going to be a problem for me in the weeks and months to come. But for now, I have to focus on the fact that I'm alive, and to make it count. I need to concentrate on the positives, because otherwise what's the point in even trying to go on?

I'm not a Buddhist, but I admire many of their tenets, including that of focusing on the moment. I've meditated for years, trying to learn to release my fears and worries. Just lately, I've lost the ability to center myself and block out everything except the peace deep inside me. And I want it back.

Some time ago, I trained in the Japanese form of energy healing called Reiki. It attracted me because it's more than just a series of hand positions and drawn symbols. It's also about concentrating on the here and now.

I say the Reiki principles softly, letting the words get carried away by the breeze.

"Just for today, I will not be angry. I will not worry. I will be grateful. I will do my work honestly. I will be kind to every living thing."

So, just for today, I'm not going to worry about what I've done. It's a beautiful afternoon, and I kissed Theo because I knew we'd both enjoy it, it would bring us both comfort and pleasure, and because I wanted to thank him for his generous gifts.

Maybe later, I can throw accusations at myself about guilt and regret and what's right and wrong.

But right here, right now, I'm going to just *be*, and enjoy the memory of his lips on mine.

Chapter Ten

Theo

In the evening, we take the woven pieces Victoria made earlier and craft ourselves a few things out of them. She makes another pillow for herself, and also a couple of baskets for carrying the eggs and taros and other food we might find. I reinforce the shelter, blocking the holes in the tarpaulin so the roof doesn't leak, and stabilizing the walls.

I'm still hopeful we might find a cave nearer the top of the island, so I don't want to spend too long on the shelter. That's tomorrow's task—to do some more exploring, collecting food and any other resources as we go.

"It's funny being bound by the hours of daylight," Victoria says as we bank up the fire so it'll hopefully last through the night. She puts another couple of taros in it to bake, and I place the single fish I caught in the rock pools onto a stick. It's a relief to have the prospect of proper food.

"Yeah," I reply, "I'm rarely in bed before midnight. But there's no point in staying up if there isn't much light." The moon is just a day or so off full, but even though it lights up the beach, we have no reading material and no TV, and it's difficult to do any crafting by candlelight.

When the food is done, we take it under the shelter, along with a couple of opened coconuts, and eat as we watch the sun sink into the sea. The sky is a fruit bowl of color—banana yellow, bright orange, and strawberry red, turning eventually to blueberry and plum. It makes my mouth water.

"I miss fruit," Victoria says as if reading my mind. "And chocolate. It's odd having nothing sweet."

"Ice cream," I say dreamily. "Mint choc chip."

"I'd even eat vanilla," she admits.

"You and vanilla? Never."

She gives me a wry look.

"I was actually referring to the ice cream," I tell her. "You've got a dirty mind." And now it's impossible for me not to think about what she was like in bed.

She was never a missionary position, lights out kinda girl. That's not to say we didn't do missionary. It was one of my favorite positions because she was always so soft under me, and I could look her in the eyes while we made love. But she liked it on top. From behind. She enjoyed being tied down. Having sex outside. Using vibrators. You name it, Victoria liked it.

And now I have to stop or I'm going to get an erection again. I'm not wearing trousers, and my boxers won't hide it. I feel a brief twinge of worry that she's going to be offended by my supposed innuendo, but she chuckles and eats the last mouthful of taro.

"I'm going to try to make us both a pair of shoes from palm fronds," she says. "I can still see relatively well."

"Anything you want me to do?"

"You could sing to me."

"I would if I had my guitar." I have a beautiful Gibson Les Paul Gold Top. I've never had lessons, but I taught myself some chords when I was a kid, and now I can strum along to most songs.

"Aw," she says, "you don't need that. You have a gorgeous voice."

I'm human enough to be flattered by her words, and give in gracefully. "All right."

She has a few of the frond panels left, so I lay them out like a mat on the sand and stretch out, then start singing one of her favorite Beatles songs. Before long, she's singing with me, and as the sun goes down, we make our way through as many Beatles' songs as we can remember, one of us filling in when the other forgets the lines.

After that, we move onto other artists, from old blues songs to rock to modern pop. The light fades from the sky and Victoria puts down her weaving and leans against the trunk of one of the palms, and we continue to sing long into the night, the fire dancing with us, and the waves providing a pleasant backing music.

The moon is high in the sky and the stars are out before I finally admit I need to stop because my throat is getting sore. "We should get some sleep," I tell her. "We're off exploring again tomorrow."

"I'm quite looking forward to it," she says as we climb into the dinghy. "I feel a bit more energetic now we've eaten."

"We'll collect as many eggs and taros as we can find and have a look for what else is growing in the bush."

"Yeah, okay."

It's not raining tonight, so I fold back the top layer of our roof and latch it back. This time we have our pillows, and we lie in the dinghy and look up at the stars.

"Are we really here?" Victoria whispers.

"It does feel like a dream."

"I guess the world is going on without us," she says. "It's funny to think people are texting and posting messages on Facebook and Instagram, talking about us."

"Maybe they're not. Perhaps nobody's even noticed we've gone."

She gives a short laugh. "Well your family will have done, if nobody else. Can you imagine what Kora's like right now? Her hair will have turned white."

I've done my best not to think about my twin sister. Kora and I are close, and although I love all the members of my family and each of my brothers the same, I feel her loss more than any other.

My family tease me about my sixth sense, but sometimes I've wondered if its existence is something to do with being a twin. We haven't exactly had the kind of connection you read about in books, where you know what the other is thinking even when you're not together, but when we're in the room, we sometimes finish off each other's sentences, and we always know what each other's opinions are going to be on something.

I picture her in my mind now, and tell her I'm alive and well, imagining I'm sending up a beacon she can latch onto so she can find us. *I miss you*, I tell her, my throat tightening. Will I ever get to see her again? And my brothers, and Dad?

"I am sorry about your grandfather," Victoria says. "How is Belle doing?"

"As you'd expect," I reply, thinking of my elegant grandmother. "Stalwart and cheerful on the outside, looking after everyone else. She'll be terribly sad now. I can't believe I'm going to miss the funeral."

"When do you think it'll be? It's Christmas Eve in four days."

I look at her in surprise. "I completely forgot."

"Maybe they'll wait until after Christmas and see if they can find you first."

"Yeah, maybe." Of course, they can't wait indefinitely. At some point, if we're not discovered, they'll have to go ahead with the funeral.

I look up at the stars, letting the emotion wash over me gently like the waves outside.

"Do you believe in an afterlife?" Victoria whispers.

"Of course. Don't you?"

"I don't know."

"You always used to."

"I've changed a lot."

I turn my head to look at her. I know she was christened as a child, and her mother used to take her to church. "You go to church for weddings and christenings and funerals, don't you?"

"Doesn't everyone?"

"You've surprised me. I thought you believed."

"I did have faith," she says. "But as I said, over the past few years, and especially over the last six months, I seem to have lost it all." She sighs.

I watch a shooting star streak across the black sky. "I have to believe. I can't bear to think I won't see my granddad again."

I stop speaking and clench my jaw. A tear leaks out of my eye and runs down the side of my face.

Victoria reaches out and brushes it off with her thumb. Then she slides her hand into mine.

We lay there like that for a long time. Eventually, her regular breathing tells me she's dozed off.

I turn my head to look at her. In the moonlight, I can't see the mosquito bites I know have been plaguing her, and the dark shadows under her eyes have disappeared. Her face looks like porcelain. Her hair is a sheet of silver.

I still can't believe she kissed me. I know it doesn't mean anything. It wasn't a signal that she wants to sleep with me, and she wasn't leading me on. It was a gorgeous afternoon, and she was overcome by the moment and wanted to say thank you for the Haven.

I kissed her back because, well, I'm a guy and I'm not going to turn away when a sexy woman presses up against me and kisses me, even when she is my ex. It was a special moment, and I need to leave it at that and not analyze it to death.

It is difficult not to wonder whether it might lead to anything else eventually, if we do remain here for a while. But we still have the huge hurdle of our past to get over first. And the more time we spend together, the greater that hurdle seems.

My eyelids are drooping. Before I doze off, I get up and bank up the fire again. Then I return to the dinghy, curl up around Victoria, and go to sleep.

*

Day three on the island, and we're starting to get into a routine. I awake to find Victoria sitting on the sand, naked, her clothes drying beside her as she makes more mats from palm fronds. I cough loudly, and by the time I emerge from the shelter, she's dressed and it's time for a couple of coconuts and some scrambled eggs as we watch the sun lifting into the sky.

It's already hot, and I pull on my shirt and trousers so I won't get burned or scratched as we explore the island. Victoria has washed the baseball cap, which she gives to me to wear, and she's made herself a conical Vietnamese-style hat from the fronds that covers her ears and gives a little protection to her neck.

She's also joined two smaller pieces from fronds and joined them together to make a kind of bag. I use the string to make shoulder straps, creating a backpack so I can carry anything we find back and keep my hands free for climbing. Victoria similarly strings one of the baskets she's made across her back. I slot my shell knife into a loop of rope I've hooked through my belt and, once we're ready, we head into the bush.

I head back to where I discovered the chickens yesterday. It takes us about half an hour. The ground is softer here, and the palms have thinned out, but the undergrowth has yet to thicken, so there's a natural clearing. We count thirteen chickens scuttling about in the bush and spot two roosters, which explains the two batches of chicks we glimpse in the trees.

"We'll have to make the most of the eggs," I say as we collect the ones we can find. "I hope we're not still here in the winter as they'll stop laying eventually—they don't lay as many eggs as domestic hens."

"If we're still here in the winter, we're going to have more problems than finding eggs," she says. "I can't bear to think about it."

"No, let's not. We can't store the eggs, anyway, so we'll have to eat them while they're fresh."

"How do we tell which ones are fresh? Isn't there something about it sinking or floating?"

"Yeah... I can't remember which though."

"No, me neither."

"We'll have to rely on look and smell," I reply. "A bad egg is going to smell off when we crack it. But they take a few weeks to get like that."

We spend quite a bit of time searching through the undergrowth, and in the end we fill Victoria's basket with twenty or so eggs, leaving the small pile that one of the hens is sitting on.

"I wonder how long they've been here," Victoria says as I lead the way onwards to where I discovered the taros.

"Who knows? Someone must have brought them here by boat. I wonder if they landed here on purpose or if they were shipwrecked."

"We haven't seen any sign of anyone else here. You think they'd have left a presence if they did land here."

"Yeah." I stop when I see the ground I dug up the day before. "Here. The taro leaves are long and heart-shaped." I show her the plants.

We discover they're spread in a band in this softer ground, and use the scallop shells to dig them up, piling them in my backpack until it's half full, which should last us a few days.

By this time the sun is high in the sky, and we stop for a coconut each before moving on.

It's hard going, because we're still low on energy, it's hot, and the ground rises quite sharply here. But we're rewarded when we circle around to the other side of the hill.

"Bananas!" Victoria gives a girlish squeal. "I don't believe it!"

I feel a rush of relief and joy I never expected to feel at the sight of a banana. "There are hundreds of them!"

"Oh Theo, they'll last for ages. Come on, help me get some down."

"Watch out for spiders, that's all."

"Oh, yes, thanks for reminding me."

"We'll use a stick to check them first."

We spend a while making sure the ripe bunches are free of spiders before I use my knife to separate them from the trees. Victoria catches them, and we put as many as we can into my backpack, which is holding together surprisingly well.

"I suppose we'd better make our way back," she says as I slot my shell knife into the loop on my belt.

"Are you sure? We haven't covered the top part of the island yet. There might be something interesting up there."

She wipes her hand over her face. "I'm a bit tired. I don't know if I have the energy."

Immediately, I'm concerned. It's probably just because she has her period, but we can't risk being ill here.

"No worries, let's get you back and we'll have a rest."

Chapter Eleven

Victoria

We make our way back down the hill through the bush. It's midday by now, the sun high in the sky, and it's very hot. I desperately miss my sunglasses. The sun is so strong in this part of the world.

I feel weak and irritable and tired, and I'm therefore not surprised when my vision shimmers and sparkling triangular patterns appear.

"Damn it," I say as we finally reach the beach. "I've got a migraine aura."

"Oh no, Vic."

I know why he's worried. When we were together, I had a migraine most months, and even though I took triptans for them, they often knocked me out for a few days. Here of course I don't have any pills, not even any paracetamol, so it's going to hit me like a steam roller.

Sure enough, the headache soon develops, it's only about half an hour later that I go into the bushes and vomit. When I come back, Theo takes one look at my face and leads me into our shelter. He makes me lie down, ensures I'm in the shade, and brings me some water.

"See if you can get to sleep," he says, tucking Watson under my arm. "And call me if you need me. I'll only be over there."

I blink away tears as he leaves me, feeling very sorry for myself. I hate that I've been unwell since I've been here. I want to ask him to stay and hold me, but I know I'm being pathetic, so I turn on my side and close my eyes. It's so hot. Oh for a fan or some air con…

I doze for the rest of the day, rousing only when Theo brings me some food. He's made a little omelet with cooked taro and coconut, and even though I still feel queasy, I'm also hungry, so I eat it all and then lie down again.

My head feels as if it has a jack hammer inside. I've never missed painkillers so much. It doesn't help that the sun is so bright, and there's no air.

It gets a little better when the sun starts going down. Theo has been pottering all afternoon, catching fish, adding bits to the shelter, but now he directs me into the dinghy, and he puts his arm around me as we lie down.

"How are you doing?" he murmurs.

"I feel awful. I'm so sorry."

"It's hardly your fault. I just wish I could make it better. If only willows grew here, we could try to boil some bark, because it's like aspirin. But I don't know enough about herbs to start trying them out on you—it might make you a lot worse."

"It will go," I reply. "Eventually. I'd forgotten how bad it can get without painkillers."

"Well try to get some sleep. Maybe you'll feel better tomorrow."

I doze fitfully through the night, woken often by my thumping head. I feel hot and sticky next to Theo, and I ache, so in the end I get out of the dinghy and sit on the sand for a while, enjoying the cool night breeze that brushes across my skin. It's so surreal, sitting on a desert island beach in the middle of the night. There are fewer insects than I would expect. The mosquito bites don't bother me as much as they did. We've also not seen any large mammals. It's so incredibly quiet, with just the swoosh of the waves for company. It's the first real peace I've known in months, maybe even in years. My head hurts, but my soul feels as if it's beginning to heal for the first time. Oddly, I think being marooned could turn out to be the best thing that ever happened to me. If we eventually get off the island.

I sit there for a bit longer, then, growing tired, I go back to Theo, curl up next to him, and fall asleep.

The next day, the headache is still there, although a little less intense than it was. Theo cooks us breakfast, then suggests I spend some time at the Haven. I walk over to it to discover he's been working on it, enhancing the woven leaf room to create a simple shade sail so I'm not in the direct sunlight while I'm sitting there, and he's put more dried grasses beneath the matting to thicken the cushion. He brings me a bottle of water, an opened coconut, and a couple of bananas, kisses my forehead, and tells me to relax while he goes fishing.

THE CASTAWAY BILLIONAIRE

I sit or lie there for most of the day, dozing and meditating, doing some simple yoga stretches, drinking a lot, and occasionally nibbling a banana. It's the most beautiful day, and I spend a while coming up with names for all the colors of the sky and the ocean—navy, indigo, cobalt, cerulean, teal, azure, peacock, lapis, sapphire, denim... I watch the seagulls wheeling overhead, and some other kind of gull diving for fish in the sea. Crabs scuttle across the rocks, and little fish swim through the shallows.

I watch Theo, too, when he comes out to the rock pools and checks the bottles for fish. He's wearing his shirt because he doesn't want his shoulders to burn, but it's undone, and the sleeves are rolled up to reveal his tanned arms. He's left off his trousers so he's only wearing his boxers. He has gorgeous legs. He has gorgeous everything, really. The man is like Tangaroa, the Maori god of the ocean, made real. I could sit here and admire him all day.

As the sun begins to go down, I rejoin him on the beach for another omelet.

"How are you feeling?" he asks as we tuck into the meal.

"Better," I admit. "Thank you. It's been lovely resting and relaxing all day. And admiring the view." He just nods; he obviously doesn't realize I'm referring to him.

"Tomorrow, I might explore the rest of the island," he says. "If you feel better, you can come with me. But you can always stay here if you need to."

"I'm sure I'll be okay. My headache's dull now, not banging anywhere near as much."

"All right, but try to get a good night's sleep if you can."

"Yes, Dad."

He gives me a wry look.

"It's still quite early," I say. "What shall we do this evening?"

"I was wondering whether you'd like to play chess, if your head isn't too bad."

My eyebrows rise. We used to play it back in the day, as it was a game we both enjoyed. "What do you mean?"

Grinning, he reaches over for one of my woven baskets, and I see he's filled it with objects for the pieces—one set made from brown and cream stones and shells, another set brightly colored. Small pebbles for the pawns, striped shells for the rooks, cones for the kings and queens, and other beautiful distinctive shells for all the others.

77

In front of us, he packs down the sand, then draws a chess board with a stick, roughing up the sand on every other square to denote the black squares. We set out the pieces, then Theo says, "You go first."

We were never any good really, but we used to play in bed, enjoying the mental stimulation after we'd worn out our bodies with our lovemaking. I'm sure he's thinking about that now, judging by the gleam in his eyes, but I ignore it and concentrate on the game.

My brain feels like it's rusted over, or like a muscle that hasn't been used for a few weeks. It's a bit slow and lethargic, but gradually as we play, the fog clears, and in the end I win.

He holds out his hand, and I shake it, smiling. "This was a great idea," I tell him.

"Your head isn't too bad?"

"No, actually. I feel a lot better now. I think all the rest at the Haven today really helped." I look out to sea. "For the first time, I feel as if my mind is clear. I've been thinking a lot about Wanderlust, and why I haven't been happy there lately. I think I need to make some changes."

"What kind?" he asks, stretching out on the sand.

"I want to move away from concentrating on the merchandise and get back to the real reason for doing it. Beth won't be happy about it, though. I'm going to have to cross that bridge when we get back."

"Surely she can take over all that if she wants to. It shouldn't stop you from concentrating on your side of the business."

"True." I find it difficult to explain how she always manages to talk me around. I'm going to have to be firm and stick to my convictions.

"You're the heart and soul of Wanderlust, Vic. It was always hard to remind you of that."

I meet his gaze, and I can see he's waiting for me to argue. I don't, though. We had this conversation several times back in the day. He always thought I let Beth push me around too much and make too many decisions for me. I used to protest, but he was right then, and he's right now.

"She's very persuasive," I say carefully, knowing he doesn't like her, but not wanting him to criticize her.

He gives a short, humorless laugh. "Yeah. Tell me about it."

"Let's not spoil things," I say softly.

His gaze caresses my face, and his expression softens. "No, let's not. Come on. We should get some sleep."

Relieved, I join him in getting ready for bed, then climb into the dinghy and curl up beside him. The sun has gone down quickly, and the moon is rising. Theo's eyes glitter in the moonlight.

"Thank you for today," I whisper. "For looking after me."

"I didn't do much."

"Maybe not, but I felt... cared for."

"I'm glad. I'd do anything for you. I hope you know that."

I study his face for a moment, then close my eyes. I grow sleepy very quickly, but when I open my eyes a fraction some time later, he's still watching me, playing with a lock of my hair.

*

The next day, I feel much better. My period seems to be over, and my headache has nearly gone. After breakfast and a swim together, we decide to explore the rest of the island.

This time, we go left from the beach, climbing carefully through the bush. It's hard going, and by the time we crest a ridge and stop for a break, I'm half regretting agreeing to come.

"We're nearly at the top," Theo reminds me when I suggest we turn back. "Let's just check the last bit."

It's impossible to get right to the peak as it's a vertical climb. But we make our way around the top section until we're almost looking down onto the Haven.

And there, tucked away behind a palm and going back into the hill, we find what we were looking for.

"It's a cave!" Theo is beside himself with joy. I can understand why. A cave means more permanent shelter, somewhere to take cover during harsh weather, and also a place to keep safe from any animals that might live on the island. So far we've only found chickens, but that doesn't mean there aren't other mammals we haven't met yet.

In front of it is a small plateau, maybe five feet wide, the perfect place to build a fire. We go in cautiously, as it's dark toward the back, and let our eyes adjust. It's not huge, maybe about ten feet wide, and fifteen feet deep. And it's then we realize that this was once someone's home.

There's rudimentary furniture here—a wooden seat and a low table, two wonky shelves still bearing half a dozen items, a big box with a lid, and a bed to one side. Clearly, it's been abandoned for some time—

the straw mattress is rotting, an old blanket and a few items of clothing are dank and musty, and there are even some remains of food that's long since decayed.

"They've been gone a while," Theo says, examining the mattress. "We'll have to clean the place out."

I go over to the shelves and pick up each item in turn. There's a simple statue of a woman carved out of wood. I can't tell if it's supposed to be a person or a goddess. A photo in a frame sits next to it. I take it over to the entrance to look at it in the light. It's of a woman sitting in a chair holding a boy who's about eight or nine years old. From the woman's hairstyle and clothing, I would guess it was taken in the nineteen-fifties. She's pretty, and she's laughing at whoever's taking the photo, while the boy looks up at her adoringly.

I undo the back of the frame, take the photo out, and turn it over. It says 'Mary and James, April 1957.'

A lump in my throat, I put it back in the frame, place it on the shelf, and examine the other items. There's a small pocketknife—Theo's going to love that. A silver cross on a chain, now very tarnished. A stub of a candle stuck in the top of a glass bottle that used to contain whisky, judging by the faded label. A hairbrush with half its bristles missing. A rusted cutthroat razor. An old, men's wristwatch, the hands still. Several bowls and cups carved out of wood, and also some rudimentary wooden cutlery. A large metal cooking pot, beaten into shape from a piece of metal probably found on the beach. And two books—Ernest Hemingway's *The Old Man and the Sea*, and C.S. Lewis's *The Lion, The Witch and the Wardrobe*.

"I think it was a man," I say, as Theo joins me to look at the items. I show him the photo. "It says Mary and James, April 1957 on the back. I wonder what happened to him. Do you think he was rescued?"

He picks up the wristwatch and brushes his thumb across the surface. "Maybe." He examines the rest of the items, then looks at the box. "Shall we see what's in it?"

"Hopefully no huntsman spiders."

"Yeah." Slowly, somewhat gingerly, he takes the lid off and puts it to one side. As he does, it tips over, and we both notice the rows of small lines that have been scored in the wood. They're made in groups of seven. I count the number of groups in a line. Fifty-two. Weeks?

There are six lines, and one line of twenty-seven.

"He was here six and a bit years?" Theo says. We stare at each other for a moment. I honestly can't think what to say to that, and neither can he by the look of it.

Eventually, we both peer at the contents. There are more items of clothing, most of which fall apart as he lifts them out. A pair of shoes, two sizes too small for Theo, two sizes too big for me. A small box. Several coils of good rope. Four more books—Nevil Shute's *A Town Like Alice*, C.S. Forester's *Mr. Midshipman Hornblower*, A Mills & Boon Romance called *New Zealand Inheritance* by Essie Summers, and Dodie Smith's *The Hundred and One Dalmatians*.

"Strange to have children's books with him," I say as Theo puts them to one side.

"Maybe they were James's," Theo replies. Then he says, "Whoa! Now we're talking!" And he picks up two bottles of whisky. They're both bear the same label, which shows they're Scottish. One has about three inches of liquid in it. The other is still unopened.

"Whisky? It couldn't be tequila?" But I'm joking, of course. The notion of having any kind of alcohol to numb the pain of our predicament makes me feel all warm and fuzzy inside.

"We can't drink this one," he says, waving the one that's been opened. "We'll keep it in case we have to sterilize a wound. But this one…" He holds up the unopened bottle, then kisses it. "You beauty."

"Would you two like to get a room?"

He grins. "Of all the things to find, whisky would have been at the top of my list."

Smiling, I take out the small box. It has a red cross on the top. I open it. "Oh, it's a first-aid box." It contains a tiny pair of scissors, some burn ointment, three finger dressings, some waterproof adhesive plaster, a couple of triangular bandages, a bottle of aromatic spirit of ammonia, and lots of Red Cross sterilized lint dressings of various sizes.

"What's aromatic spirit of ammonia?" Theo asks, examining the bottle.

"It's used for fainting, like smelling salts. This box is so good—it's not going to cure disease, but it's going to be really helpful."

We both sit for a moment and look around the cave. "I wonder who he was," Theo says.

"I'm guessing Mary was his wife and James was his son." I look at the first-aid box in my hands. "If he was shipwrecked here, why did he have this box? I can't imagine it washed up on the beach like this. And how about the books? He obviously didn't find those on the sand."

"Maybe he was a fisherman and his ship hit the rocks. So he had all these items onboard. And he was so excited when he was rescued, he forgot to collect them."

"Mmm. Or maybe his wife and boy died, and he couldn't bear to be without them, so he sailed off to an island to live out his days and died here."

"That's depressing," Theo says. "I prefer my version."

"I don't think he'd leave the photo behind."

"So where is he now? If he died of old age, or even of sickness, he would probably have stayed in here, wouldn't he?"

We both look around again warily, but there's no sign of a body or bones.

"Do you think we should use all these items?" I ask doubtfully. "It feels a bit… ghoulish."

"Absolutely we should," Theo replies without a pause. "There's no way I'm letting that whisky go to waste. Come on, when we're rescued, would you mind if the next person to land here stayed in our shelter or used our knife? I wouldn't."

"That's true. Speaking of knives, did you see the pocketknife?"

"I did. I'm definitely taking that."

"So do you think we should move up here?"

He goes to the cave entrance and looks out at the view. "I do. We're in the rainy season, and it's likely we're going to have bad weather at some point. I think we should try to make the place comfortable for when the weather turns. Make sure we have food up here, and dry wood so we can have a fire just outside. We need to keep a signal fire going if we want to be spotted, plus we have to be able to cook the food."

"I feel sad about abandoning our shelter," I say. "And the Haven."

"We can still go down to the beach during the day. I'll need to so I can fish. If we climb straight up from the beach, it'll probably only take us half an hour to get here. It's not that long a journey each day."

"All right."

Theo seems unperturbed about staying in a place that was previously occupied. I feel a little uneasy about it, but I'm not sure why, and it's certainly not going to stop me sheltering here. I suppose it's because I don't know what happened to the man. If I knew he'd been rescued I might feel better. But if he died here… I swallow hard.

"Come on," Theo says gently. "Let's start clearing it out and making it our own."

So we spend about an hour clearing the place out. I make a rough broom from twigs and I clear out the rotted straw from the old mattress. Theo gets rid of anything else we can't use. I start collecting dry wood to store in the corner of the cave, and pile some up for the fire on the plateau, which is protected a little from the elements by a line of palms.

When I eventually go back in, Theo has placed all the man's effects in the large box, except for the knife, the books, the first-aid box, and the bottle of whisky, which he puts on the shelf, and he's slid the large box to the back of the cave.

"Should we bring up all the woven mats you've made?" he asks.

"We could bring the pillows up, but I can make more up here. And the raft is going to be too heavy to drag up."

He nods. "We'll have to tie it to the trees to make sure the wind doesn't whip it away when the weather gets wild."

I have trouble imagining how bad it's going to get. Sometimes we catch the tail end of a cyclone in New Zealand, and parts of the country have had bad flooding and high winds. Wellington is often windy, but I've never been in a cyclone. I'm alarmed at the thought of having to cope with that here, without any emergency services and no nice, safe house to hole up in.

"All right," Theo says, "let's get going. We've got a lot to do."

We leave the eggs, taros, and most of the bananas here and head back to the beach. Theo cuts down the undergrowth as we go, trying to make a decent path we can find when we come back, and I tie bits of red string around the trees to mark our way.

When we get to the beach, we pause for a drink and a banana to keep our energy levels up, then get to work. First we tie down the dinghy to the nearby palm tree. Then we gather up all the bits and pieces we think will be useful in the cave, including the rope, the pillows, the hair clips, and Watson the rabbit, and put it in the baskets and Theo's backpack. Then we make several journeys up to the cave.

We're on our way down for the third time when Theo points to the west. I stop and shade my eyes, seeing thick gray clouds gathering.

"The weather's going to turn soon," he advises. "We should get a move on."

We return to the beach for the last bits and pieces. By this point, the wind has started to whip the sea into white horses, and the palm trees are beginning to swing in the breeze. I walk carefully over the rocks to the Haven. I've hardly got any use out of it, but I know if I don't remove the shell mobiles they'll be lost to the wind, so I take them down carefully, bring them back to the beach, and put them in my basket.

"I won't be offended if you leave them here," Theo says with amusement.

"I want to keep them," I protest. "I like the sound they make."

"All right. I've collected a few fish from the rock pools. The sun's getting lower, so we should probably get up to the cave and make a fire."

He's wrapped the top of a long, solid stick in a piece of cloth and doused it with some of the whisky from the open bottle. Now he touches it to the remains of the fire, and it leaps into life. Holding the torch aloft, he leads the way back up the hill to our new home.

It's starting to get dark by the time we've arrived and unloaded our stuff. Theo lights the fire to one side of the cave entrance, making sure it's away from the palm trees, and I collect some more dry wood, conscious it's not going to be dry for much longer. I also collect a heap of palm fronds for weaving.

As the sky turns the color of rust and the sun sinks into the sea, we go into the cave and try to make it comfortable. We've managed to bring up some of the woven squares, and we lie these on top of grasses we've collected. It's not exactly a soft mattress, but it's better than the rocky cave floor.

We put the taros, eggs, bananas, lemons, and coconuts we've brought with us to one side of the cave in our 'kitchen', while Theo places the four fish he caught in the basket near the entrance because of the smell. We put one of the fish and some taros on the fire to cook, and I begin to scramble up two of the eggs.

We eat our dinner sitting in the cave entrance, warmed by the fire, the wooden table between us. It's growing dark, but there's enough light for me to read by, so I pick up Essie Summers' romance.

Written on the first page is a short message.

To Mary, Happy Christmas, with all my love, Henry.

"He gave her the book," I say.

"I forgot that some people write in them," Theo replies. He leans over, picks up *The Lion, The Witch and The Wardrobe*, and opens the cover. Sure enough, there's another note in the front, this time in childish writing. James Cavendish.

"Henry, Mary, and James Cavendish," I murmur. "That's brought them all to life. Essie Summers was a New Zealand romance author. It makes me think they were from New Zealand."

"Yes, the names seem to suggest that." Theo pulls the bottle of whisky toward him. "Maybe we should toast them."

My lips curve up. "Yeah, maybe we should. Is the whisky definitely going to be drinkable?"

"It's unopened and it's been out of the sun. It'll be fine."

"How are we going to get the cork out?"

"It's a stopper rather than a wine cork." He gets the penknife and scores around the wrapper at the top. Then he gradually eases the stopper up until it comes out with a satisfying squeaky pop.

He lifts it to his nose, sniffs it, and exhales with a satisfied *aahhh*. He offers it to me, and I give a cautious sniff. It smells like whisky.

"Go on," I prompt. "See if it's poisoned."

Giving me a wry look, he tips the bottle up and takes a sip. He swirls it around his mouth and swallows. Then he meets my gaze, his eyes lighting up. "It's perfect."

He gives it to me, and I have a big mouthful and swallow. *Ooohhh*, talk about firewater; it burns all the way down to my stomach. I'm not a whisky drinker normally, but needs must, and I have another mouthful before passing it back to him.

We're not having many calories considering how much physical work we've done, and we're both super tired from the long day. The sun has now set, and the only light comes from the full moon that's almost hidden behind clouds, and the fire that's leaping up into the night.

"I'll bank it up," Theo says, and he places some of the bigger logs on it that'll take longer to burn.

A few drops of rain land on the palm tree in front of me, so I gather up all our bits and pieces, we retreat into the cave, and lie down on our beds.

"We need to work on these," he grumbles, trying to get comfortable. "I feel like the Princess and the Pea."

"I'll try to work out something we can stuff with grass." I lie on my side and he does the same, and we study each other in the firelight. "It's a weird feeling to think of Henry Cavendish lying in here, thinking of his family."

"For six-and-a-half years." Theo sighs.

"Do you think he died here? If we were to search every inch of this bush, would we find his skeleton?"

"I don't know. He could have been rescued, or made a raft and tried his luck on the ocean."

"Leaving behind the photo of his wife and child?"

Theo doesn't answer. I think he knows, the same as I do, that Henry must have died here somewhere.

Theo reaches out a hand, and I slide mine into it. The whisky is having an effect, and my eyes are drooping.

Within five minutes, I'm asleep.

Chapter Twelve

Theo

When I wake on the morning of Christmas Eve, it's still raining, and the sky is gray and miserable. I feel stiff from lying on the hard matting, and I sit up and stretch to try and get the aches from my bones.

Victoria isn't in the cave. I know she rises early, but where is there to go during this weather? Thinking maybe she's gone around the corner for a pee, I roll onto my front, prop my hands on my arms, and look out at the view.

Christmas Eve. This time last year I was with my family, although we weren't really celebrating, as Mum had died only a few months before.

I try not to dwell on her death because it makes me too sad, but I let myself think about her for once, wondering whether she's watching over me, maybe talking to Granddad, discussing how I'm doing. Can she see the future up in Heaven? Does she know whether Victoria and I will be rescued?

Grief is a powerful emotion, and it's hard to fight it as it swells inside me. I give in to it for a while, missing them both, and letting myself be conscious of the gaping hole their absence has left behind.

But I'm lucky in that I've never suffered from true depression, and after a while I'm able to wrestle the melancholy back down deep inside me where it belongs. I refuse to let negative feelings overwhelm while I'm here. I need to stay strong and positive for both of us.

Victoria still isn't back. I get to my feet and head to the mouth of the cave.

Here I realize how busy she's been while I was sleeping. She's kept the fire going, and about half the taros we collected yesterday are roasting there, and so are all the fish. I'm guessing she's worried we wouldn't be able to cook anything if the rain puts the fire out. She's placed the plastic bottle halves we brought up with us outside, and they're now mostly filled with rainwater, while the big plastic tank has a few inches in it. She's also woven a couple more squares which are leaning against the inside of the cave.

I pick up one of the plastic bottles and have a long drink of rainwater. Oh, that's good. Crisp and cold.

I'm guessing she's either gone down to the beach or she's off collecting food or palm fronds. I'll give her a while longer before I start worrying.

I go around to the other side of the cave, into the bush, and there discover what we didn't notice yesterday. A tiny stream, trickling down through the undergrowth and out of sight. It might not even have been here yesterday; maybe it only sprung into life with the steady rain.

I'm not sure whether we should drink it, but it'll be perfect for washing. My trousers are in the cave, but I take off my T-shirt and boxers and wash them, then take them back to the cave and spread them out on the rocks by the fire to dry. After collecting the wash box Victoria made for me, I return to the stream and wash as best as I can with the lemon leaves, then chew some mint and brush my teeth.

My bristles are getting longer and less itchy now, beginning to turn into a short beard. I've never grown one before, preferring to be clean shaven, but there's not much hope of doing that here. I'm not going anywhere near a cutthroat razor.

The rain is coming down hard now, and I stand in a small clearing and let it run over me, tipping up my face to the sky. It feels good to be clean, and it wipes away the last remnants of sleep. I feel alert and fresh. It's not going to be an easy day, especially if the weather stays bad. It's a time that should be shared with friends and families, and we'll feel their absence more keenly, I'm sure, than at any other time.

But at least we're not alone. Someone or something guided me to Victoria that day on the plane, and they also told me to stay in the seats near the emergency exit. Was it a person? My mother, my grandfather? A deity? The sixth sense my siblings tease me about? Or just my instincts? I don't know, but whatever it was, I'm thankful for it.

Standing in the forest, with only the rain to hear me, I lift my arms and call out softly, "Kia ora!" As well as a Maori greeting, it's also a gesture of appreciation.

"Oh!"

I turn at the sound of Victoria's voice behind me. Her eyes widen, and she spins away as she sees I'm naked.

"Theo!"

"What?" Amused, I lower my arms and walk up to her. "I'm just having a wash. I found a small stream."

"Oh, that's great. Um… what… how…" She stops, and as I circle her, I see the flush spread across her cheeks. "Will you please put your clothes on?"

"They're drying by the fire." Laughing, I go back to the cave and collect them. They're not dry yet, but I pull them on anyway. "If I get chafing, it'll be your fault."

"Well you could have warned me," she grumbles. "I heard you say something and thought you were looking for me."

"I was going to if you didn't come back soon," I say, smiling. I remember how I felt when I saw her naked on the beach. Clearly, she's going through something similar.

"I went to see if there were any more eggs," she replies.

"And?"

"Yes, I found four more. I thought we could heat some water in Henry's pan. We could boil the eggs, then maybe make a kind of soup with them, the taros, and the fish. I'm not super keen on the fish, but I think it's probably good to have the nutrients. And now we have bowls and spoons, so it'll be easier to eat."

"A Christmas Eve meal?"

She smiles. "Yeah, maybe."

So we set to it, munching on bananas and coconut for breakfast while we work. Victoria boils some of the older eggs, then chops them up and adds them to the hot water. I remove the cooked taros from the fire, mash a couple and add the flesh to the soup, then return the skins to the fire to crisp a bit before we eat them. I flake the fish as much as possible and add that, too. We chop up some seaweed and sprinkle that in. Then we leave it to bubble in the pan and thicken while we turn our attention to the cave.

We gather the grasses we dried the day before and stuff it into our mattresses. We use the woven panels to create a screen that should keep the worst of the rain out of the cave if the wind gets up. We collect more palm fronds and leave them by the fire to dry. Tip all the water from the smaller bottles into the tank, then put the bottles out again.

Finally, around what we think is lunchtime, we scoop some of the soup into Henry's wooden bowls and eat it while we sit at the mouth of the cave, looking out at the view.

"Not bad," Victoria says.

For a while, we talk about how we spent Christmas as a child, about gifts we've given and received, and food we've made and enjoyed. While we're talking, she hangs up the shells I strung onto string, then takes some of the palm fronds and tries to make some other decorations out of them, and even manages some chains which we string up across the roof.

By this time, the wind has gotten up, so we wash up our bowls, then retreat into the cave. We store the rest of the cooked eggs and taros in the basket.

"The fire's going to go out," Victoria says.

"We can have some of the embers just inside and try to keep a tiny fire going. We just have to be careful we don't asphyxiate ourselves."

"What about a signal fire?"

I sigh. "I'm guessing if the weather's this bad, they won't be flying, so it won't matter much."

She doesn't reply, just turns away to start doing some more weaving. I make a small fire just inside the cave entrance, hoping the smoke won't blow inside, then come back in and sit on my bed.

"Are you okay?" I ask.

She nods and continues with her weaving, eyes down.

I pick up the Hornblower book, lie near the fire, and begin to read.

It rains all day, unrelenting, sub-tropical rain, the skies heavy with gray clouds. As the afternoon wears on, the wind gets up, the palm fronds whipping about. I'm glad we're not still down on the beach. At least here we have some protection from the elements.

There's no point in going out and getting soaked, so we spend most of our time in the quietness of the cave. Victoria makes half a dozen more mats, then declares her hands are aching. The inside fire is working quite well, and I think providing I keep it relatively small and near the entrance, we should be able to keep it going. It gives us a little light, and while it's humid and hot so we don't really need the warmth, it is oddly comforting.

We don't talk much. Victoria is quiet, and I think she's upset because the signal fires on the beach and outside have gone out, so there's little chance of us being spotted, even if someone were to fly a plane overhead. I think maybe the isolation and fear is starting to get to her, which is understandable. A while ago she spent some time studying the first-aid kit, and I'm sure the thought of getting sick or injured is preying on her mind.

As the light begins to fade, I take out the bottle of whisky and two cups and place them between us. "Time for a drink," I tell her.

She sighs. "I'm not sure it's a good idea. When I'm melancholic, it only makes me worse."

I pour a small amount into the cups. "Then we'll have to do our best to un-melancholic you."

"That's not a word."

"It is now." I pass her a cup. There's a shot-sized amount in it. "Down in one," I announce.

She gives a short laugh. Together, we knock the whisky back in one go.

She coughs, and I whistle. "That's so strong," she says hoarsely.

"Good though." I pour us both another shot. "And again, down in one."

"Are you trying to get me drunk?" She says it wryly, maybe a little playfully.

"Yep." I grin to show I'm not serious, although a little of me is. I think on a night like this, it will help to blot out our predicament with more than a little whisky.

We drink that shot, both cough, then have one more.

"All right," she protests. "I need a break."

"And it's time for dinner anyway. Come on, let's dish up."

We serve ourselves some of the stew, which has now thickened pleasantly, and eat it sitting on our beds.

"I miss bread," Victoria says. "Probably more than anything."

"What about chocolate and coffee?"

"Good point. Except chocolate and coffee. Hmm, if we dry the coconut and grind it between stones, we could make coconut flour. We won't have yeast, but we might be able to make a kind of flatbread."

"That would be amazing. We'll give it a try when the rain stops."

"Okay." She looks brighter at the thought.

I'm already feeling the effect of the whisky, and I'm sure she is too. I study her fondly. She's sitting cross-legged on the bed, wearing just her T-shirt and panties, because it's so warm. She's braided her hair and pinned it up in a circle on the top of her head. She looks younger than her twenty-eight years, fresh-faced and beautiful.

Outside, there's a flash of lightning that temporarily lights up the cave. Victoria counts under her breath, getting to eight before we hear the low rumble of thunder in the distance. The rain is steady, and our water bottles are already full.

"Time for a drink," I say. I pour a small amount into each cup and pass one to her. We knock it back together. "I'd kill for some ice," I tell her.

"A margarita," she says dreamily, as I pour another shot. "Tequila, orange liqueur, and lime juice, shaken with ice, and with salt around the edge of the glass. When we get back, I'm going to get crazily drunk on margaritas."

"Sounds good to me." I gesture at the cup, and we both knock the whisky back.

She coughs and puts her hand over the cup. "We should slow down or I'll be comatose in half an hour."

"Your point being?"

"That's probably not a good thing."

"Why not?"

"I… don't know."

"Exactly." I push her hand away and pour another shot. "It's Christmas Eve and we're stuck on a Pacific Island in the middle of nowhere with very little chance of getting rescued. I think we're allowed to have one night of drunken debauchery."

"That's a good word."

"Thank you. I quite like it."

We both down the whisky.

"Whoa." She blinks slowly. "That stuff works fast."

"It's good whisky. I bet Henry paid quite a bit for it."

"I wonder what happened to him," she asks, a tad wistfully.

"Let's pretend a passing fishing ship spotted his fire and took him home to where Mary and James were waiting for him with open arms." I pour another shot.

"I have a sneaky feeling it didn't happen like that."

"Me too, but it's Christmas, and I'm making the rules tonight." I knock back the drink.

She turns the cup in her fingers, her gaze lingering on me. "You look different with a beard."

"Different how?"

"You're normally very swish."

"I don't know what that means."

"It's British. It means smart and fashionable. Elegant. But with the beard you look quite..." She licks her lips. "Rugged."

"Rugged good or rugged bad?"

"Just rugged. Rough." Her eyes gleam in the firelight.

I gesture at her cup. She knocks it back, and I drink mine too.

"Mmm," she says. "I feel... loose. Alcohol's like a wrench, isn't it? It loosens all your nuts that have been over tightened."

"My nuts are fine just the way they are, thank you very much."

She chuckles. "I noticed."

That makes me laugh. "You shouldn't have looked."

"The way you didn't look when you saw me each morning on the beach?"

"Ah."

"Yes, ah. You think I didn't know you were watching me?"

I don't say anything, just meet her eyes and let my lips curve up. Then I lean forward and pour us both another shot.

"We should ration it," she says. "We might be here for some time and be glad of it."

"Fuck that. It's Christmas Eve."

She sighs. "Fair enough." We both down the shot.

I put the cup on the rocky floor. Outside, lightning flashes again, and this time she only gets to six before thunder rumbles. Immediately after, the rain seems to get heavier, if that's possible, hammering on the leaves. Inside, though, it's warm and dry, and the alcohol has given me Dutch courage.

"I think it's time," I tell her.

She blinks. "Time for what?"

"To talk."

Her brow lowers. "About what?"

"About us. Come on, you knew it was coming at some point. We've got to do it. And we're stuck here, so neither of us can walk off in a huff."

Her smile has faded, and her eyes have turned stony. "I don't think that's a good idea."

"I do."

"It's Christmas Eve."

"We've got to do it, Victoria. We could be here for some time, and it's the elephant in the cave, blocking out the light. We've got to clear the air."

"What if we can't?"

"We have to try. But we must have some rules."

She runs her tongue over her teeth. "What kind of rules?"

"We're going to have a talking stick." I pick up a small branch from the pile of firewood. "When one person has it, the other can't interrupt. We need to let each other speak. We also have to listen and be open-minded. And lastly, we have to be honest."

Her eyes flicker with emotion. It's too dark for me to read it, but something makes me think it's fear. "Theo… it's been such a long time. We've been doing all right, haven't we? Why spoil it now?"

"I don't want to spoil it. I want to make it better."

"Better how? We're talking, and the atmosphere is pleasant. We're getting along."

"I want to do more than get along." I sigh. "I didn't think I'd ever see you again, and so I tried to move on. But God, or Fate, or whatever you want to call it, has brought us back together again, and something inside me is absolutely convinced we're not going to get off this island until we sort it out."

"That's just you being fanciful," she says, although there's no scorn in her voice.

"Maybe. But it's how I feel. So will you go along with it for me? And see if we can clear the air once and for all?"

She swallows hard. "All right."

The relief I feel is so strong, I have to catch my breath. "If you like, you can start," I say. "And then I'll tell you my side of it all." I pass her the talking stick.

"And I have to be honest?"

I nod.

She turns the stick in her fingers. "Okay. Maybe it's time I told you everything."

Chapter Thirteen

Victoria

Seven years ago

I stand by the window, looking out at the busy streets of Wellington. The sun has already dipped below the high-rise buildings, and although it isn't yet dark, the light is fading, and my apartment is cast in shadow.

My phone buzzes, and I look down, not sure if I'm relieved or disappointed to see it isn't Theo. It's just Beth, telling me she'll be about twenty minutes if I want to wait to get an Uber Eats together.

I dismiss the text, then glance at the one below it that I received earlier. It was from my aunt Julia. She's not strictly my aunt, she was my mother's best friend, but I've always called her auntie.

It was an innocuous text, asking what I want for my birthday, but I've been in a strange mood today, and it's stirred up memories and emotions about my mother I try to keep locked away.

I don't have my mother's suicide note. After the coroner returned it to me, I struck a match and burned it.

Now, I regret it a little, but the words are engraved on the inside of my skull, and I'll never forget them.

She told me how devastated she was about my father's infidelity. And she asked Julia to look after me, because she was the only person she trusted.

I look back out of the window, resting my forehead against the glass.

I don't know why I've been thinking about it today. I suppose because of Julia's text, and also because I have my own best friend to think of, and the absolute last thing I want to do is cause her any pain.

I feel as if I'm standing on the middle of a see-saw, and I have no idea which way it's going to tip. I thought I had my life planned out. Beth and I have finished our degrees—mine a bachelor of health, hers in business management. Just under a year ago, we bought plane tickets to Europe, and we've booked accommodation in the major cities, rail and bus tickets, and an itinerary that makes me breathless just to look at it—London, Paris, Madrid, Berlin, Prague, Venice, Rome…

She sourced the most expensive video camera she could afford and I treated us to a top-of-the-range laptop, so we can upload my yoga videos wherever we are in the world and get our YouTube channel going right away.

We created the Wanderlust Yoga website, organized a free gift for signing up to the mailing list, created Facebook, Instagram, and Twitter accounts, and we've worked hard on our branding to make sure everything has the same logo and look. We're all ready to launch our new business into the stratosphere.

And then, on a strange whim, I changed the day I normally go to the gym, and I met Theo.

I breathe onto the window and draw a heart in the steam. How could I have foreseen that? He was running on the treadmill, dressed in shorts and a gray vest, a dark V stain on his front, his hair damp at the temples and on his forehead. All hot and sweaty and gorgeous. I couldn't help but stare. And then he looked at me with his bright blue eyes, and that was it—I was lost.

We met in the foyer afterward, got chatting. Flirted. Had a drink in a bar down the road. Went back to his apartment. And ended up in bed. The first time I'd ever slept with a guy the first day I met him.

The sex was fantastic. The next day I could barely walk, and my stomach muscles ached from all the orgasms he'd given me. He asked to see me again, but I refused, conscious of my promise to Beth that I wouldn't fall for anyone and blow this chance to make something of ourselves while we're still young and without responsibilities.

But I hadn't known then that he was incredibly rich. He paid the guy on reception to call him when I came back into the gym, and he arrived ten minutes later and stood in front of the cycling machine watching me until I agreed to talk to him. He dragged me into the corridor and kissed me until I was breathless, and told me he'd continue kissing me until I agreed to go on another date, because he couldn't stop thinking about me. And I said yes, because when a man like Theo Prince tells you he's crazy about you, there's little you can do to resist him.

At first, I didn't tell Beth I was seeing him, making sure to meet him at his place during the day, and never to stay overnight. It was the first time I'd ever kept anything from her, because I was sure she'd go ballistic when she found out.

To her credit, when I eventually plucked up the courage to tell her, she just looked surprised, then gave me a hug and said of course she didn't mind—I was her best friend, and she was glad to see me so happy. I said I thought she'd be worried I'd change my mind about traveling, and she replied of course not—she knew that wouldn't happen because we'd been planning it for so long, and we'd both agreed our careers had to come first before either of us settled down. Mr. Gorgeous would still be there when I got back, she said with a grin.

I didn't contradict her. But the problem is that Theo is the best thing that's ever happened to me, and it's just starting to get good, and the last thing I want to do right now is leave him and travel around the world. I'm going to miss him terribly.

But it's not just that. We've only been dating six months, which is nothing, and even though I'm sure he'd say he'd wait for me, he's young and gorgeous and rich and with a sex drive that could power the whole of Wellington for a fortnight. How likely is it that he'd stay celibate until I came back?

I turn away from the window and walk through the apartment to the bathroom. I've been wrangling with myself for weeks, trying to decide what I'm going to do. But clearly, Fate decided I wasn't in enough turmoil, and She arranged to throw a monkey wrench in the works.

I pick up the white stick resting on the hand basin and turn it over. It says "Pregnant. 2-3 weeks."

"Fuck." I sink onto the toilet seat and put my face in my hands. I can't believe it. Oh my God. Oh my fucking God.

We've used condoms all the way. But I know they're not one hundred percent accurate, and Theo is very… energetic. One must have broken.

Tears leak through my fingers. It wouldn't be so bad if we hadn't had a conversation about our future a couple of weeks ago. We'd just had sex and were cuddled up together while the rain lashed at the windows. He was telling me about some marketing scheme he'd set up at Prince's Toy Store, and how he was going to visit the UK and Australian branches of the company and swap ideas with them.

I asked him playfully if he could ever see himself settling down with a mortgage and two-point-four kids.

"Maybe one day," he said. "A long way in the future. It'd be a disaster right now though, wouldn't it? We've got to do our best to make sure it doesn't happen and put our careers first, don't you think?"

"Of course. It was just a joke."

He nuzzled my ear. "I'm up for a lot of practicing, though." And that was the last we said on the matter.

I didn't think about it much because I agreed with him, mostly, even though, if I'm honest, a teeny tiny part of me was a bit disappointed that he didn't declare undying love and tell me he couldn't wait to have a family with me. But we hadn't been dating long, and it was far too early in the relationship to get all heavy about it.

And now I'm pregnant, and it's absolutely the worst thing that could have happened. What the hell am I going to do?

I need to get my act together, to clean my face, have a stiff drink, and think carefully about what to do. But for some reason I can't stir myself. I can't stop crying. And I'm still sitting there when Beth comes in.

"Vic?" She calls my name a few times, then I hear her footsteps coming up to the door. She knocks. "You in there?"

"Yes."

"You okay?"

"No."

"What's up?"

I give a loud sob.

At that, she opens the door and comes in. "Oh no, what's the matter?" She drops to her knees beside me.

I look at her pretty curly brown hair, her warm brown eyes that are always full of smiles, and my heart breaks.

I lower my hands and look at the white stick on the hand basin. She follows my gaze, stares, then gingerly picks it up and reads the message. She closes her eyes.

"I'm sorry." I cover my face with my hands. "Oh Beth, what am I going to do?"

"Hey, come on, it's not the end of the world." She puts her arms around me. "You silly arse. We'll sort it all out. Come into the living room, will you?"

I let her lead me to the sofa, and she sinks down beside me, her arms still around me. "I can't have it," I say, sobbing. "Theo said it would be a disaster if I got pregnant."

"He might have said that, but he's crazy about you," she insists. "I'm sure he'll come around to the idea."

"I can't have a baby now. We've got everything planned. And I want to have a career, I really do."

"We'll sort it out," she says desperately. "It doesn't matter."

But of course it does matter, and I'm absolutely gutted.

"You have to tell him," she insists after I've sobbed for ten minutes straight. "You need to talk it over with him. Text him now and ask him to come around."

"I can't. I can't face him right now. I need some time to think about what I'm going to do." I need to get it clear in my head before I talk to him.

"All right. Can I get you anything?"

"Have we got any chocolate?"

She chuckles. "I don't think so. You want me to go out and get some?"

I give her a wistful look. "Would you? I could really do with a bar of Dairy Milk right now." It's a partial truth; I could do with some time on my own. "I don't know what I'd do without you," I whisper as she pulls on her jacket and collects her purse.

She comes over and kisses my forehead. "Aw. We're besties. That's what I'm here for. I won't be long." She slips out of the apartment and closes the door behind her.

I lay back on the sofa, my head spinning. What am I going to do? I can't think straight.

If I tell Theo I'm pregnant, what will he say? Understandably he doesn't want to be tied down at this stage of his life. Equally, I know he's religious. He's not going to like the idea of me having an abortion. He's oddly old fashioned too and he's said in the past that it's best for children to have both a mother and father around. Will he want us to get married?

Marriage and babies with Theo Prince. The idea sparkles in my mind for a moment. And then I come back to earth with a bump. Even if that were to happen, he'd be full of resentment towards me for tying him down. And what about me? What about what I want? My career is poised on the edge of taking off. I know it's not impossible to have a baby and a career nowadays, but I couldn't travel around Europe and do everything we've planned to do with a newborn in tow. I just couldn't. I'd be throwing it all away. Can I do that to Beth? To myself? After all the plans we've made.

But can I really go into a clinic and ask them to rip the baby out of me?

I go around and around in circles, as the daylight fades and the room slowly becomes dark.

What am I going to do?

Half an hour goes by, and I start to wonder where Beth is. Finally, I hear her key slot into the lock and turn. I sit up, only then realizing how dark it is, and I flick on the lamp beside me. She comes in and lets the door close, and then, to my surprise, leans back on it. Her hand rises and she presses her fingers against her lips. She's trembling.

"Beth?" I get to my feet. "What is it?"

She's as white as a sheet. She comes forward, and her eyes are glistening. "I'm sorry," she whispers. "I'm so sorry."

"What's happened?" I note that she's not carrying anything. "Did you get to the shops?"

She shakes her head. "I went to Theo's office."

I stare at her. "What?"

"I don't know why. I thought I might talk to him first, tell him how crazy you are about him. I... I wanted to help..."

"And? Did you talk to him?"

She swallows hard and a tear rolls down her cheek.

"Beth!" I snap, scared now.

"He was standing by his car... And he was..." Her chin trembles again. "He was kissing someone. Vic, I'm so sorry."

I couldn't have been more stunned if she'd slapped me around the face with a wet fish. "What? Who?"

"I don't know who she was. She had dark hair, quite tall."

I feel instantly nauseous, but my brain tries to fight it. "Was it, like, a peck on the cheek?" My voice sounds pathetic, even to my own ears. "Could it have been a friend?"

"It wasn't a peck, Vic. He had his tongue down her throat and his hand on her breast. They weren't just friends." She looks distraught.

"I feel terrible. I walked up and down for ages trying to decide whether I should tell you."

My chest heaves. Then I run into the bathroom and vomit into the toilet.

I heave and heave until there's nothing left. Then I sit on the toilet seat again and cry.

Beth comes in and puts her arms around me. I think of my mother, and Julia, and my hateful father, as my life crumbles slowly around me.

*

It's a couple of hours before we hear a knock at the door.

Theo has texted me several times and rung twice, but I haven't answered. I know he's going to start to worry; I always reply to him within minutes of a text, and I've never ignored his call.

"I can't talk to him," I say to Beth, my heart immediately beginning to race.

"I'll deal with him," she says firmly. She goes to the door, while I stand in the middle of the living room, my hand covering my mouth.

Beth looks through the peephole. "It's him," she whispers.

He knocks again. "It's Theo," he calls. "Victoria? Is everything all right?"

My stomach is churning, and my heart bangs on my ribs.

"She's busy," Beth calls out. "She can't see you tonight."

"Beth, open the door, will you? I just want to know what's going on. Why hasn't she returned my texts?"

"She'll call you tomorrow. Go home, Theo."

There's a moment of silence, and then he bangs on the door, making us both jump. "For fuck's sake, let me in! What's wrong? Why won't she talk to me?"

To my alarm, Beth unlocks the door and opens it a crack. "She doesn't want to see you now," she whispers furiously. "Go away."

He looks past her and sees me, and he immediately tries to get past Beth, but she puts her arm out to stop him. "Victoria!" he yells. "What's going on? Why won't you talk to me?"

"Theo," Beth snaps. "She knows."

He glares at her. "Knows what?"

"That there's someone else."

"What are you talking about?"

"I saw you," she says, beginning to get angry herself. "Kissing that dark-haired bitch by your car. She's done with you, Theo. It's over."

He stares at her. Then he pushes the door open and marches past her.

"Vic." He stops before me. "This is crazy."

"I want you to leave," I whisper, backing away and holding up a hand as he takes a step forward.

He stops. "I don't know what she's talking about."

"She saw you, Theo. With that woman. Kissing her."

"I've been in a meeting for hours," he says. "I haven't been kissing anyone."

"I don't believe you."

He looks over his shoulder at Beth, who's standing a few feet away, her arms folded across herself defensively. I'm so relieved she hasn't left. I couldn't do this by myself.

"She's mistaken," he says. "She saw some other guy, not me."

"I was ten feet away and it was full daylight," Beth states bitterly.

He returns his gaze to me. "She's mistaken," he repeats. "It wasn't me. I wouldn't do that to you."

I wish I could believe him, but I don't. Emotion whirls inside me like clothes in a washing machine. "You're rich and gorgeous. You could have any woman you wanted. And I'm supposed to believe you've settled on me?"

He gives me an incredulous look. "I'm crazy about you. Why would I throw away the best thing that's ever happened to me?" He's an amazing actor. He's almost believable.

But all I can see in my mind's eye is the night my mother accused my father of being unfaithful. They'd assumed I was asleep in my bedroom, but I heard everything, including his insistence that he'd done nothing, insinuating Mum was crazy for even thinking it. And then, hours later, his final admittance that he'd had an affair.

"Stop it." Tears tumble over my lashes and pour down my cheeks. "I want you to go."

He clenches his fists and his eyes blaze. "I've thought of no other woman for the past six months. I thought you knew me, understood me. Do you really think I'd cheat on you? On any woman? You think I have it in me to do that?"

"I have no doubt at all that any man would, given the opportunity." I believe it with all my heart and soul.

I can't bear this. I feel sick, and I can't stop thinking about the little life growing inside me. I don't want to tell him about it. I don't want him to think we have a connection, because we haven't—it's been broken irrevocably. He's broken it.

"I want you to leave," I state, angry when my voice wavers. "Please, just go."

"You're making her feel unsafe," Beth says. "If you don't leave now, I'll call the police." She has her phone in her hand, her thumb hovering, ready to dial.

Theo looks from her to me. He doesn't anger easily, but at the moment he looks livid. "All right," he says, "I'll leave. But I'm not going to let this go."

He walks past Beth and out of the door. Once he's in the corridor, he stops and turns, obviously about to say something.

But Beth closes the door, cutting him off.

Chapter Fourteen

Victoria

Present day

"Wait," Theo says. "What?" His face shows complete shock. "You were pregnant?"

I bite my lip. Then I give a small nod.

"But we used condoms."

"They break, Theo. It happens. No contraception is a hundred percent effective."

Silence falls between us. Lightning flashes, and thunder follows after I count to four, a deep booming rumble that travels through the rock and up into my bones.

"Why didn't you tell me?" he whispers.

"Because you cheated on me."

He looks at his cup, finishes off the whisky inside, then pours himself another. He doesn't offer to pour me one.

I feel a twinge of guilt at my flat accusation. We're supposed to be clearing the air, not throwing hand grenades at each other. "It wasn't just that," I add softly. "I was sure you'd be against me having an abortion, and I needed to make that decision myself."

"Is that what you did? Had an abortion?"

"No. A week later, I started bleeding and miscarried. I was only six weeks anyway. It wasn't exactly a baby." I stop as a sudden wash of sorrow fills me and my eyes prickle with tears. I sniff and rub my nose. "It still gets me, even now."

Theo studies me for a long time. "I'm sorry," he says eventually.

"For what?" I don't want his sympathy. Telling him about what happened has brought it all back—all the indignation and hurt I've tried to put behind me all these years. "For cheating on me?"

"I didn't cheat on you," he says.

I blow out a long breath. "I thought we were going to be honest with one another."

Seven years ago, in the days following that dreadful evening, he tried to ring me, then sent me texts and emails when I refused to answer. I deleted them all without reading them, but it was impossible not to glance at the subject line, most of which said something along the lines of: *I didn't do it!*

He picks up the talking stick, then gives me a wry glance. I press my lips together and lean back against the wall. "All right," I say. "You tell me your side of it. I won't interrupt."

I know this is going to be hard. I have no doubt he's going to try to defend himself and somehow excuse his indiscretion, if I can eventually get him to admit it. I can remember my father's list of explanations. It started with *She was just a friend, it was a goodbye kiss. You're making too much of it.* Then it progressed to *It was just the one time. It didn't mean anything.* And it ended with *I'll never do it again. I promise.*

"That day," Theo begins, "from about two o'clock I was in a meeting at the office with Dad, Ben, Lucas, Jacob, and Kora. We were going through a marketing plan for a new range of action figures. I texted you around five asking if you wanted to come over in the evening, but you didn't reply. You always replied within minutes. And suddenly, I knew something was wrong."

He sips his whisky. "There was no reason for it; you'd probably gone out with Beth and your other friends, or you were at the gym, or maybe even doing some yoga. But I couldn't get rid of this nagging sense of anxiety."

"Your sixth sense?"

He gives a ghost of a smile. "Maybe. So I slipped out of the office and walked down to your apartment. It was the first time I'd left the office since about midday, when I nipped out to get a coffee from Starbucks."

I frown and open my mouth to say something. He waves the talking stick at me, so I close it again.

"I went to your apartment, and eventually Beth opened the door. When she said you knew there was someone else, that she'd seen me with another woman, I pushed past her because I had to see you, to know whether you really believed I'd do something like that. I could see immediately that you did believe it. And I knew then it was all about your mother."

Indignation makes me gasp. "Bullshit!"

He points the stick at me and snaps, "Back then you refused me a trial and you acted as both judge and jury and condemned me. I have the right to defend myself."

I glare at him, my chest heaving, but don't say anything.

"You'd told me what happened to your mother, and that your mother's best friend looked after you, but you didn't talk that much about it. I thought it hadn't affected you that much, but I saw then how wrong I was. You believed—believe, because I don't think you've changed—that all men are unfaithful at heart. That we can't help ourselves. But you're wrong. I didn't kiss anyone that day. I didn't cheat on you, Vic. I wouldn't do that—to you or to any other woman."

"Beth was ten feet from you," I say bitterly. "She clearly saw both you and the woman. And if you're thinking of changing your story and saying it was Kora or a friend, apparently you had your tongue down her throat and your hand on her breast."

"I'm not changing my story. I didn't do it."

"You did! For fuck's sake, tell me the truth!"

He hesitates then. "The truth?"

"Yes, Theo! I want to hear it from your lips!"

He turns the stick around in his fingers. "Are you sure?" he asks softly. "It's going to change everything."

"What are you talking about? Of course I'm sure."

"Okay." He has another sip of whisky, then leans forward and pours me a cup.

"I don't want any more."

"You're going to need it." He sits back. "Do you remember asking me to leave?"

"Yes, of course."

"I walked out into the corridor."

"Yes, and you turned and were going to say something, but Beth shut the door."

He nods. "What I never told you was that when I looked at Beth, she was smiling."

I blink. "Smiling?"

"Yes."

Thunder rolls around the cave again. My brain is fuzzy and refuses to work. "She was glad you'd left the apartment. Relieved."

"It wasn't a smile of relief. It was a smug smile of victory. I've never been completely sure, but after what you told me tonight, I'm convinced. She knew you were falling for me. She was already worried you were going to say you'd changed your mind and didn't want to travel. And then you told her you were pregnant. I'm guessing you said I wouldn't be happy about an abortion. So she made up the story about seeing me with another woman because she knew it would ruin our relationship. After what happened with your mother, there's no way you'd believe me over her. And with me out of the way, she'd be able to convince you that having a baby was a bad idea, and encourage you if you said you wanted an abortion."

I stare at him in horror. "You're wrong."

He doesn't say anything.

We stare at each other for about a half a minute.

Eventually, my head spinning, I say, "If that's what you believed, why didn't you tell me back then?"

"In the beginning I tried, but I'm guessing you deleted my texts and emails without reading them. And eventually…" He hesitates, and for the first time he looks away, out of the cave, past the fire into the rainy night. "I knew it was over between us. You'd chosen her over me." His gaze comes back to me. "You were all set to go traveling. You had everything planned. And I didn't want to spoil that for you. I hated Beth for what she did, but I wasn't going to destroy your relationship over it. I decided to let you go."

I feel nauseous. I don't believe him. "There's no way Beth would do that to me," I whisper furiously. "She's my best friend. She's been by my side since we were eleven, supporting me. I love her dearly. She wouldn't do that." I believe one hundred percent in our sisterhood. She'd die for me, and I for her.

"Why would I lie to you now, after all these years? What's in it for me?"

"To get in my knickers if we're stuck on this island?"

"There's that," he admits, brief amusement making him smile. Then it fades. "I'm sorry." There's pity in his eyes. "I've been battling with myself as to whether I should tell you. So much water has passed under the bridge now. But over the past few days, I've seen how much pain you're still in. What happened between us nearly destroyed us both. I didn't date anyone for a year. I was gutted, because I was crazy about you. It's always eaten away at me that I've never been able to defend myself. I hate the fact that you think I cheated on you. I wouldn't. I couldn't. I loved you. I still do." He gives a little smile.

"Stop." Tears fill my eyes. "We shouldn't have talked about it. We could be here a long time, and now you've spoiled it by accusing my best friend of something so horrible I can't even…"

"Vic, do me one favor. For one moment, stop hiding behind the barriers your mother's death erected, and let yourself think about it. Let yourself accept for a second that it might be true. Just consider the fact that I didn't cheat on you. Just think about it."

I don't want to. I want to run away. Out into the darkness, away from him. But it's late, and it's dark and pouring with rain, and the bush is filled with creatures, and I don't want to go out there.

I'm stuck here, in this small space. There's just me, the quiet darkness, and Theo.

The flickering fire casts our moving shadows on the walls. It feels prehistoric, as if a medicine man is drumming, calling the forces of nature down upon us.

I meet Theo's eyes. Then I close my own.

I feel as if I'm standing on the beach below us, about to let the sea wash over my feet.

Slowly, I let the first wave touch my toes.

What if Theo never cheated on me?

I haven't for one second ever considered that, but I promised I'd talk to him tonight, and so I do as he bids and pretend for a moment that he's innocent.

What if, that terrible night, he hadn't been lying when he insisted he'd been at work all day?

The first he'd have known about it was when he came up to the apartment. It would explain his obvious shock, and his resulting anger. I'd remembered my father's outrage and had assumed Theo was faking his out of guilt. But what if it had been genuine? In the six months I'd known him, I'd only seen him get angry once, when a couple of teenage guys had bumped into an old lady in the high street, and had laughed as she'd stumbled. He'd caught the old lady and made sure she was okay, and then he'd ripped into the boys and made them apologize.

He said he'd never cheat on me because he loved me, and not only that, but he'd never do it to any woman. I've always assumed every man is weak and has the capacity to cheat because they can't help themselves. But what if I'm wrong? Is it possible that some men are decent enough that, even if they're presented with the opportunity to cheat, they'd say no? Have I been wrong all this time?

I force myself to look at it objectively, which I've never done before. What kind of man is he? Since we've been on the island, I have to admit he's shown himself to be a good, kind, decent, guy. When we were together, he never showed me anything except love and adoration. I'd thought he was different because he never gave me any sign that he was like my father.

Not until the moment Beth told me she'd seen him with another woman.

I open my eyes. He's watching me, one half of him lit by the dancing flames, the other side in shadow. He looks rough and rugged with his dark beard. I can easily picture him going out and killing a saber-toothed tiger to bring back to the cave for food.

What if he didn't cheat on me? Is it at all possible?

I look in my heart, and I realize it is.

Joy is the first thing I feel, and it must show on my face, because the corners of his lips curve up in response.

And then the implication of that hits me, and my smile fades.

Beth.

If I accept Theo is innocent, it means Beth didn't see him that evening.

"I know," he says, obviously following my train of thought. "I'm so sorry."

"It doesn't mean she did what you said," I say. My voice sounds tight and squeaky. "Maybe she saw another guy who looks a bit like you. She could have really thought it was you."

"Maybe." He doesn't mention her smug smile, but I know he's thinking about it.

Beth isn't here to defend herself. I need to talk to her about it, to listen to her side of things if I'm about to accuse her of something so terrible.

Although I didn't do that with Theo.

The shame of it hits me with full force, taking my breath away. I didn't want to listen to his explanations because I felt in my heart he must be guilty, and everything he said would be a lie designed to absolve him from his terrible act.

I never gave him a chance to defend himself. To tell his side of things. If he truly didn't do it… How must he have felt at such an accusation? At having his girlfriend assume he was capable of acting like that toward her?

If he is innocent, it's possible Beth orchestrated the whole thing. She could have lied about seeing Theo with another woman because she was afraid I was having doubts about our plans, and the pregnancy brought her fears to a head.

I want to cry bullshit. I can't bear to think she's been my friend for all these years, and yet she did something so horrible it makes me want to weep.

Is she capable of doing something like that?

In my heart, I know she is.

As the notion settles into my brain, I realize that horrifically, catastrophically, it's probably true.

I didn't tell her about meeting Theo until we'd been dating for about a month because I thought she'd go ballistic. I suspected she would be terrified he'd change me. Outwardly, she didn't react like that, but it wouldn't surprise me if inwardly she was devastated.

It doesn't mean she planned it all. It could have been a spur of the moment thing, when she went out to get me chocolate. It doesn't mean she's proud of it, and doesn't regret it. She cried with me when I had the miscarriage and looked genuinely distraught. It doesn't mean I chose a cruel, heartless woman over a loving man all these years. I can't let myself think that—it's just too horrible to contemplate.

But it does mean it's my fault Theo and I broke up, because I was too blinkered to even consider the truth. I know what happened to my parents affected me. But now I recognize that the tendrils of distrust went even deeper than I'd thought.

It explains why I didn't even consider it might be Beth behind it all. At the time, with my hormones all over the place, I could never have entertained the idea that the man was innocent and the friend guilty.

It explains it. But it doesn't come close to excusing it.

Chapter Fifteen

Theo

Victoria puts her face in her hands, her elbows resting on her knees. "No," she whispers. "Oh God, no, no, no."

She believes me. Joy, relief, and furious triumph rush through me at the same time. I feel as if I've been pushing a massive boulder up a mountain for the past seven years, and all of a sudden I've crested the hill and come to the top.

"It can't be true," she says. "You're wrong. You have to be wrong."

I don't say anything. I don't have to. She knows it all now. I can see it's sinking in. She just needs time to process it.

She lowers her hands and stares at me. Her pupils are wide in the semi-darkness. Her face is white. "You gave me the speech about me being judge and jury, and condemning you when you didn't have a chance to defend yourself. So you know what it feels like. I can't do the same to Beth. It wouldn't be fair."

"Fair?" Anger rushes through me. Absolutely it would be fair for Beth to get her comeuppance for throwing a fucking grenade into my life. Why should she get the chance to worm her way out of it and convince Victoria she's innocent?

But I've promised myself I won't get angry. I know the bond between best friends is often long-lasting and deep, and it's going to be even harder for Vic—who has the relationship with her aunt Julia to put into the mix—to think the worst.

"I get your point," I say carefully, forcing my fists to unclench. "I know you'll want to hear her side of it. All I wanted tonight was for you to be open to the possibility that I didn't do it. I know it's made you miserable, and I'm sorry about that, truly I am. I didn't do it for any other reason than because I couldn't bear the way you looked at me as if you hated me."

"I did," she whispers. "For a long, long time." Her hand comes up to cover her mouth. "If you didn't do it... It means I ruined everything."

"Beth ruined everything. Your reaction was understandable considering what you'd been through, both with your parents and the fact that you were pregnant." I feel a sudden stab of sorrow. "I'm sorry you lost the baby."

"It was a fetus, not a baby." But for the first time, a tear rolls over her lashes and trails down her cheek. She wipes it away and bites down hard on her bottom lip.

"I'm sorry I said it would be a disaster if you got pregnant. I was young and stupid. But I did love you. I would have stood by you."

She meets my eyes then. "I know."

We fall quiet, and for a while the only sound is the rain lashing on the trees and the rolls of thunder. Victoria has a mouthful of whisky and shudders. I lean my head back on the cave wall, watching the shadows moving on the rock.

"I've never considered you could be innocent," she says eventually. "Not once. In the beginning, I couldn't see past what my father did. And later..." She frowns and looks into her cup. "I think there were times I felt a flicker of doubt. Things Beth said... did... but I wouldn't let myself contemplate what she might have done, because it was too horrific to consider the implications."

"What kind of things did Beth do?" I ask.

She turns the cup in her fingers, and she's silent for a long time before she finally answers. "She's the most loyal person I've ever met. Ever since we were at high school, she's stood by me. Wanderlust Yoga was her idea. I had the idea of doing online classes on YouTube, but it was her idea to make it a travel program too. And all the way, she's been the driving force behind the company. She's amazing at organization. She's driven and ambitious. She makes all the deals, does all the business side of it. But she's never tried to step into the limelight. She's always been careful to make it all about me."

"I know you owe her a lot," I say gently.

"I do. But over the years, there have been times when I've felt..." She struggles to find the words. "Manipulated," she settles on. "I haven't always agreed with her decisions, but she manages to talk me around. She's very skillful at making me feel as if I'd be stupid not to go with whatever she's suggesting. Does that make sense?"

"Kind of."

"I'll give you an example. Last year, during lockdown, we were both stuck in our apartments. And she announced she'd gotten a deal with a Kiwi TV channel who would do a live broadcast of my Yoga routine every day, a kind of 'look after yourself during lockdown' thing, shown against a background of cities and other places, to continue that Wanderlust feel."

"I remember," I say, because I watched her every day while we were at level four and confined to our own houses.

"I didn't want to do it," she admits. "I didn't like the pressure of doing it live on TV. I'd have to film it myself, and I like to be able to edit my videos before they go out. But when I said no, she said something like, 'Well, it's up to you of course. I'm sorry, I just assumed you'd want to help all those people who are stuck indoors, especially the mums with kids who'd love to watch the famous Victoria. They'd get so much out of it. But, well, you know best.' She made me feel bad at the thought of refusing."

It doesn't surprise me at all that the calculating Beth knows exactly how to wrap the gentle, sensitive Victoria around her little finger. But I just nod and say, "Do you think she'd realized you hadn't been right since your accident?"

"I do. I think that's why she took Lucy on." She hesitates, then says, "The argument about the TV show wasn't the only disagreement we had."

"Oh?"

"After the accident, when I broke up with Jack, I was struggling. I canceled a few appointments, and I was late for a couple of videos. I was in a lot of pain with my shoulder, and I was just plain miserable. I wasn't feeling very Zen. I was lonely, and I kept…" Her gaze meets mine for a moment. "I kept thinking about you," she says softly.

Me? I assumed she hadn't given me a single thought since I walked out of that apartment.

"I felt very sorry for myself. I could have done with some mollycoddling." She gives me a wry smile. "But Beth took the other approach, and she gave me a big speech about how I had to pull on my big-girl pants. We didn't argue exactly, but I felt resentful and went quiet, and I think she knew she'd pushed me too far. Not long after that, she took on Lucy and said Lucy was going to take over some of the business organization, because she felt she'd lost my trust. I felt terrible. And now... I think that's why she did it."

She finishes off her whisky and holds the cup out for more. I slosh a small amount into it.

She has a mouthful, her eyes meeting mine. I don't look away, and we sit on our beds, studying each other.

"You really didn't do it?" she says eventually. Her voice sounds almost wistful.

I shake my head. "I swear on my grandfather's life." That makes her press her fingers to her lips as emotion overwhelms her. "Why would I?" I continue. "You were perfect, everything I'd ever wanted. I was crazy about you. I was..." I hesitate. Should I tell her? It'll only make her feel worse.

"What?"

"Nothing."

"Come on. We promised we'd be honest with each other."

I sigh. "I was going to ask you to marry me."

Her jaw drops slowly. "Seriously?"

"Seriously. I'd even bought the ring. White gold, two carat solitaire. I think you'd have liked it."

She gives a short laugh. "Two carats? Yes, Theo, I'd have liked it. Did you use it to propose to Emma?"

"Nope."

"Why did you break up with her?" She looks curious, and a little ashamed. I think she might have assumed I cheated on her.

"She said I was too defensive. That I wouldn't let her in. I tried, but... I was worried about getting hurt again."

Victoria falls quiet again for a while as she processes that. I know I've virtually said it's her fault that I'm still single. It's harsh, but it's true. If we're being honest with one another, she might as well know everything.

She's studying me, and she blinks slowly, the first sign that the whisky is getting to her. "You were really going to ask me to marry you? We'd only been dating for six months."

"Yup. I had it all planned. I was going to take you to Lake Wanaka and propose. It was all booked."

Her eyes turn shiny in the firelight. "Oh Theo. That makes me so sad."

"I'm sorry."

We both finish off our whisky. The alcohol is running through my veins now, and I feel loose and relaxed. My anger has faded away. Like Vic, all that's left is sadness.

"Would you have wanted me to give up our plans for traveling?" she asks eventually.

"Of course not. Europe is only twenty-four hours away."

"I didn't have the money back then to fly here, there, and everywhere. I couldn't have flown back to you very often."

"I would have come and visited you, wherever you are. I'm a billionaire, remember?"

She purses her lips. "I'd forgotten that."

"Or I'd have waited for you until you came back, if you had rather I'd done that."

"Do you think you could have waited?"

"I'm a grown man, not a dog."

"Maybe, but you were a very lusty young man. Could you have gone without sex for six months, or however long it took me to return?"

"I have a right hand, don't I?"

That makes her laugh.

"I'd have done anything for you," I say simply. "That was part of the problem, that you could assume so quickly that I'd been unfaithful. Maybe I should have fought harder to defend myself, but I was so hurt… I kept thinking fuck her, if she didn't trust me, she doesn't deserve me. Then I'd drink half a bottle of whisky and pass out on the sofa. Dad was quite worried about me at the time."

Her eyes are definitely shiny now in the firelight. She swallows hard, fighting against her emotion.

Our lives have been ruined, and all because of one woman who was terrified I'd get in the way of her plans.

"Is Beth with anyone?" I ask.

She nods. "She's been with Gareth for a few years. He's an odd guy, very quiet. She walks all over him. She likes to control people. I guess that's why you and she clashed sometimes."

"She was always very bossy. I didn't like that."

"No, you didn't like being told what to do."

"Still don't."

She chuckles.

I look out at the wild weather. The wind is whipping the leaves of the palms around. Every now and then, it blows a spray of rain into the cave across us. It's so warm that it's welcome, although I hope it doesn't put the fire out.

I get up and put some more branches on it, hoping it'll last through the night. Then I replace the plastic bottle halves we've emptied so they'll fill up again. The water tank is nearly full, too, so we'll be okay for water for a while. I bring in two of the full bottles and give one to Vic, and we both have a big drink.

We sit in the entrance to the cave for a moment, looking out at the stormy sky. "Somewhere out there, Santa is getting his sleigh ready," she whispers.

"I'm sorry, I don't have a present for you."

"Aw, Theo. You've given me the best present I could ever have asked for."

Her words give me a warm glow. "We should get some sleep," I say. "It doesn't look as if the storm's going away anytime soon."

"Okay."

So we both return to our mattresses and stretch out, turning on our sides so we're facing each other. We're about three feet apart.

"It's so hot," Victoria says. "I feel as if I'm breathing underwater."

"Yeah, the humidity's probably a hundred percent."

She closes her eyes, and I close mine for a few minutes. My head is full of the conversation we've had this evening, though, and I'm not surprised when I open my eyes again to find hers open too.

"It's weird," she says, "but things really do take time to sink in, don't they? Like a stone in a barrel of honey. It's all going around in my head, and it's like with every passing second, everything becomes a little clearer."

"It takes time to process news. The implications take a while to filter through the synapses."

She reaches out a hand, palm up. I smile and slide mine into hers.

"All that time," she whispers. "Seven years. We could have been married with a couple of kids by now."

"Yeah."

"Do you think Beth planned it all, or was it a spur of the moment thing? Do you think she ever regrets what she did?"

I think of the way she smiled at me before she closed the door that night. It chilled me to the bone then, and it's chilled me every time I've thought about it since. I have no doubt in my heart that she planned it, and I doubt she has any regrets at all.

But I just say, "I don't know."

"I'm going to have to talk to her about it when we get back."

"I guess."

She's quiet for a while. The flames from the fire have subsided to a warm red glow. Her eyes are two dark glassy orbs.

"Do you think we will be rescued?" she murmurs.

"I do, now we've had this conversation."

She gives a little laugh. Then she closes her eyes.

I think of my grandfather, and wonder if he's watching over us here. If he's pleased I've cleared the air.

Maybe now he'll send Dad to find me.

I close my eyes too, and drift off to sleep.

Chapter Sixteen

Victoria

I jerk awake as a deep boom of thunder rolls through the cave. It's so loud it travels through the rock and up through my body, and I'm sure it even makes my teeth rattle.

"Wow, that was loud." Theo's voice in the semi-darkness also makes me jump.

I sit up, looking out at the lightning flashing over the sea. "Have you been asleep?"

"Yeah, I dozed off for a while. Can't have been for long though. It's still dark."

"What time do you reckon it is?"

"No idea. Two a.m.? Three?"

The lightning flashes again, and I crawl to the front of the cave and peer out. I can't see the trees or the beach or the ocean, or anything in fact, until the sky lights up again, bathing the view in an ethereal white. It's only a few seconds before the next flash happens, and so it continues, only seconds apart.

"Stroboscopic lightning," Theo says, joining me on the ledge. "The Norwegians call it *kornmo*. It means grain ripener, and it happens in summer."

"How on earth do you know that?"

"I dated a Norwegian girl. She taught me a few words. Mostly rude ones."

I glance at him, watching his features flare with silver as the lightning flashes. It's funny to think of him dating over the years since we broke up. Picturing him with other women gives me a funny feeling in my tummy.

He pulls one of the mats toward him and sits on it, leaning back against the outer wall of the cave, knees drawn up. "This is so surreal. I have to keep reminding myself I'm not dreaming."

"I know. Marooned on a desert island with a gorgeous billionaire somewhere off Fiji. Some women would think that was paradise."

He chuckles. "And others would think it was hell."

"Aw, not me. I've never thought that." It's true. Even though I knew it would be difficult, I was still pleased I was stranded with him and not a stranger.

"Want to go back inside?" he asks, tossing a branch on the fire and making it flare temporarily.

"No, I think I'll sit here for a while and watch the storm." There's something fascinating about it. But it is cooler out here, with the rain blowing across us every now and then, and I wrap my arms around myself and shiver.

I should keep my distance from him until I've had a chance to speak to Beth and really think about what I've unearthed tonight. I can't just fall into his arms because he's told me he's innocent, and believe everything he's said. I'm full of conflicting emotions—sadness, anger, resentment, embarrassment, and shame, all whirling around inside me, and I need time to process it all and discover how I feel about both him and Beth.

But I'm tired, and a little drunk, and more than anything I want some comfort from a human being, and as I'm stuck on a desert island with Theo and there's nobody else here, I guess he'll have to do.

"I could do with a hug," I say. Surprise flares briefly on his face like the lightning in the clouds before he holds out a hand. I move across to sit in front of him between his legs, and curl up against his chest as he puts his arms around me.

It's not a chore to cozy up to his warm body, and we sit there for a while watching the lightning, which is truly breathtaking. The clouds light up every few seconds, and occasionally threads of light snake across the sky. There's no more thunder, and even the rain seems to lighten a little. But the lightning continues, flash after flash, tearing the sky apart.

"Maybe it's your Granddad trying to communicate," I say.

I feel more than see his laugh. "It did cross my mind."

My head is resting in the crook of his neck, and my hand is on his chest. He's only wearing his boxers, and his skin is damp from the rain. His heart beats steadily beneath my fingers.

"What was the name of your Danish girl?" I ask.

"She was Norwegian, and her name was Eir." He pronounces it 'air'. "She was a Norse goddess of healing and medicine."

"Your girlfriend?"

He chuckles. "No, that's who she was named after."

"Why did you break up?"

He sighs. "She went back to Norway. She was only here for a few months, and we were only together for a few weeks."

"You didn't consider asking her to stay?"

"No, it was never that serious."

"I bet she was serious about you."

"Nah."

"Was she blind?"

He laughs and kisses the top of my head.

"There hasn't been anyone else serious?" I ask him.

He sighs again. "No, Vic. Only you."

"Not even Emma?"

"Not really."

He was going to ask me to marry him. I feel a twist of regret deep inside. I can't help but feel anger toward Beth for destroying that.

I know I should wait until I talk to her before I condemn her. But the thing is, I know Theo's telling the truth. I just know it in my heart. All these years something has felt wrong inside me and I haven't been able to work out what it is. And now I know, and it feels as if a huge weight has been lifted.

"I'm sorry," I whisper.

His hand stills where he's been rubbing my arm, although he doesn't say anything.

"I wish…" My voice trails off. I can't bear to voice it.

He rests his lips on my hair, and we sit there like that for a long, long time.

My mind wanders, tired from the whisky and lack of sleep. How different it could have been if we'd stayed together. Maybe he'd have helped out with my business, or at least been there to support me. Perhaps we'd have kids. My hand strays to my belly as I think about my miscarriage. I've tried not to think about having Theo's child growing inside me, but it's impossible not to imagine it now.

And as for the sex… I've hardly been with hundreds of guys, but I've had a few partners, and Theo was by far the best in bed. I think it was because he was so attentive, and he didn't mind spending hours kissing or touching or playing with toys to arouse us both. He used to love going down on me, and I can remember stretching out on his big bed and feeling as if I was floating on a cloud as he teased me with his tongue and fingers.

He shifts, jerking me out of my reverie, and I realize he must be growing uncomfortable on the hard ground, even though he has a mat.

"Do you want to move inside…" I stop as I feel the reason for his discomfort. Something long and firm is pressing against my right hip.

I lift my head and look at him.

"Sorry," he says. "I have very little control over it."

"Are you thinking saucy thoughts?"

"Might be."

"Me too," I confess.

His eyebrows rise.

"You were so good in bed," I tell him.

His lips curve up. "You weren't so bad yourself."

"We were fairly compatible, weren't we?"

"We were very compatible. I seem to remember a particular weekend where we spent all day and evening in bed."

"I was just thinking about that," I say softly.

His eyes flash briefly in the lightning, and the desire in them gives me goosebumps.

This guy has been amazing since we've been on the island. He built me the Haven, found me food, and looked after me, and I don't for a second believe he did it because he thought I'd sleep with him if he did. He's a decent guy who's been treated abysmally, and although I know the whisky, the late night, and the storm have more than a little to do with it, I want to show him how sorry I am, and how much I wish things could be different.

So I reach up and press my lips to his.

He inhales, the same way he did at the Haven, but he doesn't pull away. His arm tightens around me, and he tilts his head to change the angle of the kiss, parting his lips. I do the same, murmuring as his tongue slides against mine, and we exchange a long, heartfelt kiss that leaves me tingling from the top of my head to the tips of my toes.

When he eventually pulls back, I stare up at him dreamily. He cups my face and brushes his thumb across my cheek.

"You're so damn beautiful," he says. Is there a touch of regret in his voice?

"And you're gorgeous," I reply. "Even with the beard."

He scratches his cheek, giving me a wry smile. "I'm not sure if it suits me. I'm kinda glad we don't have a mirror."

"Me too," I say fervently. "And I would like to apologize for the fact that I haven't washed with anything but lemon leaves since I've been here."

"You smell of summer," he whispers.

My gaze drops to his mouth. "Will you kiss me again?"

"Are you sure?" His deep voice sounds husky with desire.

I nod. And so he lowers his head and touches his lips to mine.

We kiss for a long time, me curled up on his lap, my arms around his neck. I can hear the rain pattering on the leaves and the sound of the ocean in the distance, and occasionally a low rumble of thunder rolls, although nothing as loud as we've heard before. The lightning continues to flash, though, as if we're making out in front of a hundred photographers who are taking our photo with their cameras.

But there's nobody else here, no one to pass judgement on us or to question why we've taken this step when so much water has passed beneath the bridge, and our future is so unsure. It's odd, but at that moment I feel as if time is meaningless, and what went before and what lies ahead are irrelevant. It reminds me of the Reiki principles I quoted in the Haven—just for now… This moment is the only thing we have control over, and the only thing worth worrying about.

And right here, right now, I'm with Theo, and he's the only thing I want, desperately, more than anything. I clutch my hand in his hair, and he mutters something and runs his hands down my back before brushing one around my ribcage and up to my breast. He lifts his head to look at me for confirmation, and when I nod, he cups my breast and strokes his thumb across my nipple.

I haven't worn a bra since we got here, and my T-shirt is damp from the rain and clinging to me, so my nipples are ultra-sensitive where they're protruding through the material. I shudder as he touches them, and then he kisses me again, for the first time turning up the heat, his mouth searing across mine.

I shift on his lap, feeling his erection beneath me, and go to get up so we can move into the cave. But Theo shakes his head and turns me so I'm still sitting on his lap, my back to his chest. He lifts my face so he can continue to kiss me, then moves his right hand beneath the elastic of my panties and slides his fingers down into the heart of me as he begins to tease my nipple with his left.

I moan as his fingers move easily through my swollen folds, and automatically arch my back as he plucks my nipple and rolls it between his thumb and forefinger. Mmm… a dull ache grows deep inside me, and I don't fight him when he drops a hand to push my legs apart to give himself better access.

It's a magical moment, sitting there on top of the mountain looking out over the ocean, lit by lightning. We both inhale as the wind blows a light curtain of rain over us, and then laugh and continue to kiss, turned on by the feel of the elements around us.

Theo slides his fingers down into me, gathering moisture, then brings them back up to caress my clit, until I'm panting with need and moving my hips to match the motion of his fingers. Behind me, I can feel his erection pressing against me, hard as the rock beneath us. I want him inside me. But when I try to move, he tightens one arm around me. He wants me to stay here; he wants to give me pleasure, and I'm certainly not going to fight him.

His fingers move more quickly, teasing me ever onward, and his other hand caresses my breast, playing with the nipple through the now-soaked T-shirt until it's like a pebble in his fingers. Then he switches to the other, and alternates between the two, while he plunges his tongue into my mouth.

It's not long before I feel my orgasm build, and he obviously senses it as well, because he murmurs, "Come for me, Vic," and almost on command my muscles tighten, and I'm consumed by the sweet, hard pulsing of a blissful climax. Six or seven strong clenches follow, leaving me breathless and limp in his arms.

"Oh…" I lean back against him, exhausted.

He kisses my cheek, my hair, and my neck, while he runs his fingers lightly up the inside of my thighs and brushes over the top of my panties.

"You feel good," he murmurs, kissing my mouth as I lift my face to him.

"You, too." I can still feel his erection behind me. "I want you, Theo."

He hesitates, catching my arm as I go to rise. "I don't know that we should."

I kneel before him and take his hands. "I know why you're saying that, but—"

"I don't want you to regret it." His voice is firm. "I'm really glad we had this conversation tonight and we've cleared the air. But I know it's made some things more difficult for you, and I'm sorry about that. I don't want to make it worse by doing something that in the morning you'll wish hadn't happened, because we can't take it back."

"I know." I realize something else then—*he* might not want to take it further. I was mean to him, and I destroyed our relationship. The argument could be made that I had good reason, but it doesn't excuse it. I didn't let him explain himself. Maybe he doesn't want me anymore. "If you don't want me now, I'll understand," I whisper.

His expression turns exasperated at that. "You're kidding me?" He looks down at his erection. "I can't fake this."

"I know, but—"

"It's not that, Vic."

"You don't want either of us to regret it in the morning."

"I don't want *you* to regret it. I would never regret it. I'm crazy about you. Of course I want you. Why wouldn't I?"

It's the final thing I need to convince myself this guy is innocent. Despite everything that's happened, he still wants me.

And I want him. So there's nothing more to be said.

Chapter Seventeen

Victoria

I get to my feet, take a deep breath, hold the bottom of my T-shirt in both hands, and peel it up my body before tossing it inside the cave. Then I slide my panties down my legs and throw them in, too. At that moment I'm glad I wax because if I was into shaving, I'd look like a gorilla by now.

The lightning flashes, showing Theo's wide eyes as he sees me naked. I gesture to his boxers. He doesn't have to be told twice, and he eases them over his erection and down his legs before tossing them in the cave.

"You want to go inside?" he asks, his voice husky.

I shake my head. I feel exultant, a part of the wild night, as if the lightning has zapped through me. I place a foot on the other side of his hips, then lower down until I'm on my knees, straddling him. Lowering a hand beneath me, I take his erection in my hand and give him a couple of long strokes. He groans, swelling in my hand. I kiss him in the semi-darkness, still stroking him, enjoying the slide of skin over his iron hardness, then guide him beneath me until the tip parts my folds. Finally, I sink down until I'm impaled on him.

His mouth opens under mine, and we go still, drinking in the moment, enjoying just being together in this intimate way. I can feel him all the way up, thick and hard inside me.

"Vic…" he murmurs, stroking up my thighs to my hips. "That feels so good…"

"I know…"

"I've missed you, baby…"

I kiss him, filled with joy at being with him again, and begin to rock my hips, driving him in and out of me. *Ohhh…* it's a blissful feeling. It's as if we've become part of this crazy night, like we're two elemental spirits, part of the trees, the rain, the lightning, sparking with electricity, smelling of the wet earth and the lemons and the ash from the fire.

"I think I'm drunk," I whisper, and giggle, and feel the curve of his lips below mine.

"Want to stop?" he asks.

"No. I'm having far too much fun." I cup his face, enjoying the sensation of his bristles on my hands, and plunge my tongue into his mouth, kissing him deeply. He sighs, leaning his head on the wall, just letting me. I like this, being on top, in control, making love to him slowly, enjoying the spray of the rain on my back, the heat of the fire on my face. His hands roam over me, stroking up my back and around my ribs to cup my breasts, where he plays with my nipples, arousing me again.

We stay like this for ages, playing with each other, enjoying the journey of arousal rather than being desperate for the destination, but neither of us were going to last forever, and eventually my hips begin to rock more quickly, driving us both closer to the edge of bliss.

"Come for me," I whisper to him, kissing his nose, his cheeks, around to his ear, and nibbling the lobe.

His breaths are coming fast, and his fingers have tightened on my hips as he drives himself up into me. Oh... I'm so close... I lift my head and we slam together, moving fast, our cries being lost in the wild night as thunder rolls around us, and lightning flickers continually in the sky.

He gets there a few seconds before I do, his fingers digging almost painfully into my skin as he shudders. I rock a few more times, then stop as I clench around him, and we sit locked together like a beautiful marble statue, until our bodies finally release us, and we exhale in a rush and a release of tension.

I bury my head in his neck, and he puts his arms around me. As the wind blows a sheet of rain across us, cool on our hot skin, we both exclaim, then laugh.

"We should go into the cave," he says. "I don't want you to get cold."

"Just a minute," I mumble. I want to hold onto this moment a few more seconds. I've never been closer to him, and I don't want to let him go, because I know tomorrow I'll be sober, and I'll have to think about what this means and what Beth did, and I don't want to. I want to just be, with him, and not think of anything except how wonderful it is to have him inside me, and how much it feels as if this is meant to be.

But nothing lasts forever, and I don't want to make him uncomfortable. So I give him one last kiss and then lift off him.

"Come on," he says. We go inside, and he moves our two mattresses together. We both lie down, and he covers us with the blanket. He gestures for me to turn onto my side and then pulls me up against him, my back to his chest. I snuggle against him, enjoying his warmth and the touch of his hands on my skin.

"Go to sleep," he whispers in my ear.

I close my eyes, and within a few minutes, I do as I'm told.

*

The next time I open my eyes, the cave is filled with golden white light, almost as if an angel has come down to visit us and is standing just outside.

Theo is still asleep. Part of me wants to wake him to share the first light with him, but I need a few minutes to myself. So I slip out of bed, go silently to the mouth of the cave, and peer outside.

There's no angel, but the rain has stopped, the clouds have vanished, and the sky has turned into a beautiful palette of golds and oranges in the rising sun. The storm has blown itself out, exhausted no doubt by its brilliant light display last night.

I pick up my wash box, slip on my frond shoes, and make my way into the bush, to Theo's stream. There I carry out my morning ablutions, scrubbing my skin with lemon leaves and shivering in the cool water, and washing my clothes and leaving them out to dry in the sun.

Not far from the stream, a semi-circle of palms rings a small clearing that looks out over the beach below and the ocean beyond that. I spend five minutes picking up dead branches and flattening the ground, then stand in the center with my palms together.

Lifting my arms, I raise my hands above my head and arch my spine back as far as is comfortable and hold that for a count of ten. Slowly, I bend at the waist until I can hold the backs of my calves for another count of ten. I slide my right foot back, feeling the stretch in my left leg, then draw my left foot back to form the plank, holding it for another ten. Gradually, I lower down until my chin touches the ground, then push up to the Cobra position and hold that, feeling the stretch in my spine and tummy. Next I push up to form the Downward Dog, and follow that by bringing my right foot forward to stretch the muscles in my bottom and legs. Finally I push up to the Standing Forward Fold, lift to the Upward Salute, and return to the Prayer Position.

I do this ten times, slowly, reverently, letting my mind calm as my body automatically goes through the Asanas. It's been a while since I've exercised, so I don't push myself, trying to find enjoyment in the stretches and the peace of the scene.

I can smell the lemon on my skin, the rich, earthy smell of the wet undergrowth, and the salt from the sea, which seems to pervade everywhere on the island. The air is warm, although the morning breeze is fresh for once, and I breathe deeply, glad the humidity has lifted, if only for a short while. Birdsong fills the trees, and color is everywhere, from the gold sunrise to the deep emerald of the trees to the azure of the ocean. A streak of red flashes in the palms too—a rosella, a kind of parrot, swooping to the nearest branch.

My last routine complete, I walk to the edge of the clearing, find a patch of ground empty of twigs and sharp stones, and sit facing the ocean.

For a while, I just drink in the view, trying to let my mind quieten. I know I won't be able to meditate properly as I have too much on my mind, but I try to relax anyway, hoping the island can help me unravel the various threads in my mind.

It's so beautiful here. Yes, it is a prison, but it's a breathtaking one, and there are a lot of worse places to be marooned. We haven't seen any dangerous animals, no crocodiles or scorpions or venomous spiders, and at least we were able to take shelter in the cave when the weather became bad.

For the first time, I let my mind dwell on the fact that we might never be rescued. It's not beyond the realms of possibility. There are hundreds and hundreds of islands and islets in Fiji, all scattered across miles of the Pacific, most of which are uninhabited. Even if a plane were to fly over our island at some point, they might not see the fire, especially if, like now, we'd let it go out on the beach, and then they'd mark us off as having been searched.

We could be here for weeks. Months. Even years.

Or we might never be rescued.

I think about Henry Cavendish, and wonder whether he died here. Is his skeleton lying somewhere in the bush?

What would happen if we were here for the rest of our lives?

Panic makes my heart race, but I concentrate on my breathing, knowing I have to deal with the truth. I might be here for a long time with just Theo for company. I need to think about that, especially after what happened last night.

I think of how he held me tightly to him as he kissed me and pleasured me. And then how I sat astride him and rode us both to a climax. I didn't really give him much of a choice. He could have thrown me off, but he's a healthy guy with a high sex drive, and he hasn't had any for a while, so he would have needed iron control to say no. And anyway, I don't think he wanted to. I think he still desires me, still wants me.

But where do we go from here, after everything he told me?

My head is in such a mess. I desperately want to believe it—and yet the connotations of what it means about Beth are so immense I can't process them. She's been my best friend for seventeen years. She's done so much for me, for the business, and if we were to get back, I don't know what would happen if I confronted her and she admitted she hadn't seen Theo that night.

It's possible she would continue to insist she saw him—what then? How would I ever know whether she genuinely thought she saw him, or whether he was lying?

I wouldn't, of course. It means I would have to trust him.

Whether we get back or whether we don't, it all comes down to that. Do I trust him? No matter what Beth's stand is?

I do. Deep in my heart, I'm convinced he's telling the truth. Beth was either misguided or manipulative. She didn't see him kissing someone else. He was faithful to me. Obviously, I hurt him badly by thinking he could have cheated, but last night seems to prove he's open to the possibility of us rekindling our relationship.

So… is it a possibility? Is that what I want?

Tears prick my eyes. It's what I want more than anything in the world.

The realization almost takes my breath away. Realizing Theo hadn't cheated on me was one of the best moments of my life. I was crazily in love with him seven years ago, and it's only taken ten days for me to fall in love with him again.

It's going to be hard for the two of us to put aside our resentment and hurt—it won't happen overnight, I'm sure. But if we're willing to work on it, maybe we stand a chance.

However, there are practical things to think about. My contraceptive injection will last for another… what… seven weeks or so? We probably need to draw up a calendar in the cave like Henry did, so we can keep track of time and I can be sure of my dates. So for seven weeks I'll be protected against pregnancy. And after that? I think Theo still has the three condoms in his wallet. And then we're out of protection.

Pregnancy is a very real risk, as I wouldn't be confident using the Fertility Awareness method. The thought of having a baby here in the wild terrifies me. I know women have been having babies—and continue to do so—in their natural habitats for hundreds of thousands of years, but I'm a modern woman with no other women to help me, and as sweet, helpful, and capable as Theo is, I doubt he's as good as a qualified midwife. We'd cope. But I don't want to just cope when I have my first baby. I want a nice clean hospital with all the right equipment and a helpful midwife to guide me through it.

Unless we cross our fingers that we'll be rescued before any baby comes along, it means sex is out of the question once I'm no longer protected.

It would be torture to be stranded on the island with Theo and not be able to touch him. But I'm not sure I like the alternative.

I hadn't realized how much stuff I take for granted in my everyday life. I choose my contraception without any thought as to how I would cope without it. And what about the health service? Hospitals. Doctors. Flu jabs. Penicillin. Telephones. Cars. The Internet. All these marvelous inventions I use every day without a second thought. Running hot water. An oven I can turn on when I need it. Heat pumps. Fans. My collection of soft throws that are tossed over my chairs and sofa for when I want to snuggle up. All my gorgeous clothes. I'd give anything to be able to go into my walk-in wardrobe and rifle through my tops. Silky underwear. Chocolate. Muffins.

I swallow hard, missing my old life so much it hurts. But I know that if we are rescued, things are going to be very different when I get back. Even if Beth protests her innocence, my relationship with her has changed dramatically. What does that mean for the business? For my daily life, going forward?

So many unknowns, and I don't know how to sort them all out in my head. And suddenly, I want Theo. I want his arms around me, his mouth on mine. He makes me feel better. I don't care what happens, I just want to be with him.

The revelation spreads through me, and it lifts my heart. I want to be with him. And now we have all this time together to get to know one another again. Seven weeks before my injection runs out! I'm damn well going to make the most of that. I hope he's ready to get his socks screwed off!

I get to my feet and start pulling on my clothes. And then it hits me. It's Christmas Day! It makes me laugh out loud. I've never spent a Christmas in the northern hemisphere, so I'm used to spending it around the pool, eating turkey kebabs on the barbecue in the hot sun. But even so, this will be the weirdest Christmas Day either of us have ever spent, I'm sure.

It's as I pull my T-shirt over my head that I first hear it. It doesn't register at first. It's way off in the distance, and it sounds like an insect.

I slip on my frond shoes and turn to go. Then I stop. I turn back to the view of the ocean.

And there, in the sky, is the object that sounds like a faraway mosquito.

It's a plane.

Chapter Eighteen

Theo

I jerk awake at the sound of Victoria screaming from outside and scramble to my feet. Is she being attacked by a wild creature? Has she fallen and broken a leg? I feel disoriented and dizzy for a moment. All night, it seems, I've been dreaming I was on the phone to Kora, and have been trying to describe our island to her so she could come and rescue us, growing increasingly frustrated as I failed to explain our location.

I pull my boxers on hurriedly and race to the cave entrance, and find Victoria jumping up and down, waving her arms as she looks to the sky.

"It's a plane!" She yells the words, her face flushed, her eyes alight.

I follow her gaze up to the sky and see to the north above the ocean a plane almost overhead. It's lowish in the sky, passing west to east. Has it seen us?

"Quick! We've got to get the fire going." I turn and run back in for the remainder of the dry firewood and bring it back to the cave mouth. Victoria is already blowing on the embers, and I put small twigs on it until the flames start dancing, then add a couple of larger branches to make it flare.

By now Victoria is waving her arms again and screaming again, even though I'm sure she knows nobody in the plane would be able to hear her. But I join her, jumping up and down, yelling at the top of my lungs, and dancing about like a madman.

The plane has passed over us now and is heading east. It gives no sign it's seen us—but then what sign can it possibly give? It could circle back I suppose to double check, but it doesn't, it flies on regardless, eventually disappearing into the puffs of white clouds that have replaced the heavy gray ones from yesterday.

It's only then I realize the storm has blown itself out, and it's a gorgeous summer day. Christmas Day.

I look at Victoria with a grin, which fades as I see tears pouring down her face. "They didn't see us," she whispers, bringing up a hand to cover her mouth.

"We don't know that. They were pretty low. They might be heading back to Fiji now to report what they saw. Come on. We've got to get down to the beach and light the signal fire there."

She nods and wipes her cheeks, and at that moment she looks so beautiful it takes my breath away. I cup her face and tilt it up so I can look into her eyes.

"They saw us," I tell her with conviction. "They'll be back later, okay? So we have to get ready."

She nods. "It's Christmas Day," she whispers, her voice little more than a squeak.

I smile. "I know. Merry Christmas."

"Merry Christmas."

I bend my head and touch my lips to hers. She holds my upper arms, then moves her hands to rest on my chest.

"Should we talk about last night?" she asks when I lift my head.

"Later. First we need to get the fire going."

"Okay." She looks around our little home. "What if they don't come until tomorrow? Do we come back up here tonight?"

"Yeah, why not? It's not far. But we should gather up anything we don't want to leave behind in case we don't get a chance to return here."

We take a quick look around. Victoria puts the photo of Mary and James Cavendish in her bag, the copy of Dodie Smith's *The Hundred and One Dalmatians*, Henry's carving, and Watson the rabbit. I take the penknife and the man's watch. We decide to take our pan down with the remaining food, but leave the bowls and spoons in the cave. We also leave our mattresses and pillows, but put on our clothes and woven shoes.

I stretch out the blanket and start moving the leftover branches onto it. "There might not be much dry wood down there."

"Good thinking." She helps me pile the branches and twigs on, and then we tie up the corners and loop a piece of rope through it so I can carry it on my back. I hold out my hand, she slides hers into it, and we begin the walk down to the beach.

It's not an easy climb, especially with all the firewood, so we don't get a chance to say much on the way. Victoria said she wanted to talk about last night, and while I make my way carefully through the wet undergrowth and the slippery rocks, I can't help but wonder what she wants to say. She responded to my kiss and didn't push me away, but that doesn't mean she doesn't regret what happened.

I don't regret it, but I feel a twinge of doubt at the wisdom of reminding myself how wonderful things could be between us. All the time I kept her at arm's length, I could tell myself I'd imagined how hot and sexy and amazing she was in bed. Our tryst has rekindled all those dreams I've had over the years of her, and proven that my imagination isn't better than reality.

And what if she tells me she enjoyed it and wants it to continue? What if we get off the island? And what if we don't? So many questions, and I have no answers for them. I guess I'm going to have to wait and see how it all pans out.

It takes us about half an hour to get to the beach. We're not surprised to find the shelter completely destroyed. The tide is going out and the beach is littered with seaweed and other detritus, more plastic bottles, and old fishing nets. We place the items we were carrying at the edge by the old shelter.

"Fire first," I tell her, and she nods her agreement.

We untie the blanket and make the fire. The sun is blazing brightly now, so I'm able to use a water bottle as a lens, and a flame leaps into life within a few minutes. Soon the kindling is crackling, and we begin to add bigger pieces to encourage it to burn.

I hope we have enough to keep it alive for a while. Most of the wood around the beach is wet. Victoria helps me drag as many branches from the bush as we can to the beach, and we spread them out to help them dry in the sun. As soon as I think they're dry enough, I heap them onto the fire so it's blazing.

With the sun high in the sky, we need to take shelter or we're going to get horribly burned. Victoria has brought her conical hat and she's put the old baseball cap on me, and I'm wearing my shirt, but she only has her T-shirt and has nothing on her arms. We've done fairly well not to get sunburned so far, so we go over to our shelter, prop it up as best as we can, and settle down to have some scrambled eggs, coconut, and bananas.

"What's the first thing you're going to do when you get back?" she asks.

"Have a soak in the hot tub with a beer and a steak sandwich."

She laughs. "You've been thinking about that, haven't you?"

"Dreaming about it, yeah. What about you?"

"The hot tub sounds good. I'll choose a glass of crisp Sauvignon, and a great big veggie burger with extra cheese and fries."

"That sounds good. I'll add fries to my order."

"And chocolate ice cream to finish."

"Apple pie for me. With heaps of cream."

"Mmm." She smiles, then looks at her banana, sighs, and eats it. "I might never eat another banana again."

"I know what you mean."

We eat quietly for a while, looking out to sea, searching for any sign of the plane returning. The sky remains clear, though, just endless blue, with puffs of white.

"Do you think they flew back to Suva?" she asks, naming the capital of Viti Levu, the main island of Fiji.

"I'm sure of it. And it wouldn't surprise me if they're going to wait for high tide."

"Why?"

"I imagine they'll bring a seaplane, and it'll be easier to get closer to shore at high tide."

She looks out at the ocean. The tide has reached its lowest point and has started to turn. "So maybe later this afternoon or early this evening?"

"I would say so."

"I wonder if anyone's waiting there," she says. "If they've even noticed we're missing!"

I chuckle. "Maybe we'll get off the plane and everyone will be, like, oh, have you been away?"

"Beth might be there," she says.

I meet her eyes. "Yeah," I say softly. "I've thought about that."

"I'm not looking forward to that conversation. I've been thinking about it a lot. I'm sure she's going to insist she saw you."

"It wouldn't surprise me."

"As I see it, either she really thought she saw you. Or she's going to continue to lie. So when it comes down to it, it's about whether I trust you, isn't it?" Her hazel eyes are wide and clear.

"I suppose so."

Her gaze searches my face. I can hear the swoosh of the waves up the beach, the cry of seagulls, I can smell the sea and the lemons nearby. But I can't take my eyes away from hers.

"I do," she whispers.

My heart lifts. "You mean that?"

"Yes. Whatever happens next, Theo, I believe you didn't cheat on me. And I hope you know how sorry I am that I screwed things up between us." Her eyes glisten.

"It's all right. It's all done now." I gesture at the dinghy. We previously dragged it out of the bush to let it dry, and now it sits in the shade. "I could do with a doze. Want to cuddle up?"

She nods and rubs her nose, so we climb into the dinghy, roll up one of the mats we have left for a pillow, and she curls up beside me, her head on my shoulder.

"Everything's going to be all right," I tell her, kissing the top of her head.

"Do you really think they saw us?"

I look out at the bright blue sky. I think of my grandfather, and my feeling deep down that he put us here until we'd resolved our differences. "I do."

"I hope you're right. I want to be rescued. But it's funny, this morning I was thinking I might have a long time stuck here with you, and for the first time I was excited by the idea."

I stroke her back and down over her hip. "Me too."

"I can think of worse things than being stranded with you, Theo Prince."

"And me with you, Victoria Sullivan."

She sighs, and within five minutes we're both asleep.

*

Our late night and the climb down from the cave must have exhausted us, because the sun is heading toward the horizon when we wake. It must be about four p.m. Victoria is still asleep, curled up beside me. I sit up, relieved to see the fire still burning, and I get up and go over to it to add some more driftwood to make it leap nice and high.

I stand at the edge of the water, looking out to sea. I was so convinced the plane had seen us. If it hasn't... Victoria is going to be deeply disappointed despite her assurance that she was looking forward to more time with me. And I'll be the same. We need to get off this island. I have things I want to do! Places to go, people to see. The break has been a lovely rest, but now I want to get going. I feel a surge of frustration. "Granddad," I murmur, "come on. I did what you wanted. I made up with Victoria. It wasn't easy, but I did it. I'm ready to go. Please." I close my eyes and let the sea breeze play across my skin. "Please..."

I stay there like that for a long time, feeling the sun on my face, tasting salt on my lips.

And then I hear it. In the distance, a quiet buzz like a faraway mosquito.

I open my eyes. There's a dot in the sky, coming from the east.

"Vic!" I yell, not wanting to take my eyes away from it.

There's a squeak in the dinghy as she sits up. "What?"

"The plane!"

I hear her scrabble to get out, and then she runs across the sand to stand beside me. She lifts a hand to shade her eyes. "Where?"

"There!"

"I can't see it!"

"To the right of that cloud that looks like a muffin."

"You've got food on the brain—oh! I see it!" She squeals in excitement. "Theo!" She turns and throws her arms around me. "They're coming back!"

"I hope so." I cross my fingers behind her, hoping it's not just another passenger flight to Fiji passing hundreds of miles away. I squeeze her hard, and then we both turn back to watch the speck growing bigger. It's definitely heading for us.

I run to the fire and pile all the remaining driftwood on it so the flames are leaping five feet into the sky. Then I run back to the water's edge where Victoria is standing, her hands shading her eyes. "It's coming!" she yells. "It's coming toward us!"

She's right. I can clearly see it's a plane now, and I was right, it's a seaplane, the two slender floats under the fuselage becoming visible the closer it gets.

Victoria is crying now, tears rolling down her face, and I well up too with emotion as the plane begins to descend toward us. It's definitely coming for us. They've found us.

I pull her toward me and wrap my arms around her, and we watch, wiping away our tears, as the seaplane lands elegantly on the surface of the ocean. It then turns in the water and heads back toward us.

I can see faces at the windows, but I can't make any of them out yet. I don't care who it is, though. Someone has found us, and we're going to be rescued.

The plane stops a few hundred yards out. We wave to them, jumping up and down, so excited it's impossible to stay still. There's a short pause as the door opens and they get a dinghy out and onto the sea. While they're doing this, the pilot takes off his headphones and sunglasses and waves through the window, and emotion rushes through me so powerful it makes tears run down my face.

"It's Ben," I whisper.

"Your brother?"

I nod. And then I see who's climbing into the dinghy, his gray hair clearly visible against the dark blue sea. It's my father. He waves at me, and I wave back, not caring that my face is wet with tears.

Another man climbs in with him, around the same age, carrying a small doctor's bag. It's Dad's cousin, Brock King. I'm not shocked to see him. We're close to the King family, and they would definitely have been involved in the search, I'm sure.

My father picks up the oars and begins rowing toward us.

I hold Victoria to me tightly, looking over my shoulder at the island. It gives me a funny feeling inside to think we won't be coming back here. It kept us safe, gave us food, and looked after us when the storm came. And it helped us work through our problems and finally move on from our troubled past.

I look back at the ocean, at my father's back as he rows toward me. Then I lift my gaze to the sky. "Thank you," I mouth to my grandfather, sure he had a hand in saving us and getting us rescued.

And then the dinghy is finally close enough for my father to stop rowing and jump out. He wades through the water toward us, and he wraps me in the fiercest hug he's ever given me.

"Thank God," he whispers in my ear, kissing my cheek and hair, holding me so tightly I think he's going to break a rib. "Oh, thank God."

Chapter Nineteen

Victoria

I watch Theo's Dad envelop him in a bear hug, tears pouring down my face as Theo is overcome by emotion. It's a beautiful sight, two men not afraid to show their feelings, and I have to admit to a little envy at their obvious love for one another.

Nick Prince is tall with shiny gray hair, a neat gray beard, and lots of laughter lines at the corner of his eyes. He moves back a little and holds his son by his upper arms. "Are you okay?" he asks fiercely. "You're not hurt?"

"I'm fine, Dad. I'm sure I smell awful and look worse, but I feel fine."

"You smell of lemons," Nick says, his voice hoarse with emotions. He clears his throat and turns to the other man, who's currently pulling the dinghy ashore. "Brock will check you both over."

"Seriously," Theo protests, "I'm fine." But he turns to greet the other gray-haired man anyway, also giving him a big hug. I remember him telling me that Brock King is his dad's cousin and a doctor. It wouldn't surprise me if he insisted on coming with Nick, as the whole family is quite tight.

Nick finally looks at me. "Victoria," he says, holding out his hands. "How are you, sweetheart?"

"You remember me?"

He smiles. "Of course I remember you."

I burst into tears again and cover my face with my hands. Nick gives me a hug. He's a little taller than his son, and he smells of a nice masculine body wash.

"It's all right," he murmurs. "You're safe now. Are you hurt?"

"No, I'm fine," I manage to squeak.

"Are you the only two on the island?"

"Yes," Theo says as I move back and wipe my face. "How many others have been rescued?"

"Thirty-seven so far. Thirty-nine including you two. Not many out of a flight of two hundred and eleven."

"The woman I was traveling with," I ask hopefully, "Lucy Rippon, I don't suppose she made it…"

Nick shakes his head, his face full of sorrow. "I'm very sorry."

I blink away tears. I'd hoped she'd made it somehow.

"Hello, I'm Brock," the other man says as he turns to me, and he shakes my hand enthusiastically. He has kind eyes that bring a lump to my throat. "It's good to see you both looking so well."

"Yeah," Theo replies, "we haven't been too bad. A bit of sunburn. Lots of mozzie bites. Victoria had a migraine, but I think you're feeling better now, aren't you?"

I nod. "Let's check you over," Brock says, placing a hand on my back and steering me to the rocks nearby, and he proceeds to take my temperature and blood pressure and make sure I'm not injured in any way.

"Ben flew the plane here?" Theo asks his father.

"Yes. The others wanted to come, but we weren't sure how many survivors we might need to take back. They're waiting in Suva."

"All of them?" Theo asks, surprised.

"Lucas, Jacob, Kora, Heloise, baby Estella, Belle," Nick says, naming his mother, "Sarah and Pete," naming Theo's other grandparents. "They all wanted to come." He looks at me and smiles. "And you have lots of people waiting for you, too."

"I do?"

"Your father's there with his wife, and everyone who works for you."

I'm stunned. "My father?"

Nick looks surprised I'd even question his presence. "Of course. He's been out of his mind with worry."

I'm shocked he even noticed I was missing, but I don't say so.

"I'm very sorry to hear about your father," I say to Nick.

"Thank you."

"When was the funeral?" Theo asks.

"We haven't had it," Nick replies. "Grandma wanted to wait for you. She was determined you'd be found."

Theo nods, but I can see he's feeling emotional again. Nick smiles and ruffles his son's hair, then turns and looks around the island. "How did it go here? How did you get by?"

"We followed Granddad's survival tips," Theo says. "Make a shelter. Victoria did some weaving with the palm fronds. Foraged for food. There are wild chickens here and we found eggs and taros and bananas."

"You didn't have trouble with the storm last night?"

"No," Theo says without looking at me. "We found a cave high up on the hill and just waited it out."

"Someone was marooned here before us," I say as Brock turns to Theo to check his vitals. "We found a few of his belongings up in the cave. I have a photo of his family with me."

"Interesting. We'll check him out when we get back." Nick gestures at the dinghy. "Are you ready to return to civilization?"

Theo and I both hesitate, then laugh. "Definitely," we say at the same time. I collect my little bag with the couple of bits we want to take away with us. But we both pause at the edge of the sea. Nick and Brock start pulling the dinghy back into the water while we turn back to look at the island.

"I feel kinda funny about leaving it," I whisper.

"Me too. I suppose it's a bit like Stockholm Syndrome."

"We didn't have that terrible a time here, did we?"

"Not at all," he says.

We study each other quietly. I want to hug him, but I'm conscious of his father in the dinghy, and whoever's on the plane watching us. I felt so close to him last night, but I don't know what kind of relationship, if any, we're going to have in the real world. When you're the only two people on a desert island, it's natural to cling together. But what awaits us now?

"Come on," he says with a smile, holding out a hand. I smile back and slide mine into his, and he leads me to the dinghy. We climb in, and Nick pushes us out and begins to row back to the plane.

"Merry Christmas," Brock says, and we both chuckle.

"Merry Christmas," Theo replies. "I appreciate you all coming out to rescue us on Christmas Day."

"We weren't even sure anyone realized we were missing," I joke.

Nick and Brock exchange an amused glance. "Then I think you'd better prepare yourself," Nick states.

"Do you mean because of the family?" Theo asks.

"Not quite." Nick pulls slowly and evenly, his muscles bunching as he slides us through the water. His gaze is half amused, half embarrassed.

"Come on," Theo says, "spit it out."

"Well, pretty much the whole world has been holding its breath, waiting for you to be rescued."

Brock nods his agreement. "Once the news came out that you were probably together, the Internet exploded. There have been so many articles about the kind of conditions you've had to deal with, how you've coped with finding food…"

"And lots of speculation about your… relationship," Nick says.

"Wait," I say. "What?"

"How did they know we were together on the island?" Theo asks, puzzled.

"One of the other survivors saw you getting into the life raft together," Nick replies. "A Kiwi paper did a story about the billionaire and the famous yoga instructor, discovered you once dated, and that was it. There's been nothing else in the news for ten days."

"Holy shit." I feel a little faint.

"Yeah," Nick says. "So you'd better get prepared. The press is going to be waiting at the port and in the capital. Lucas has organized some security and a car to pick you up and take you to the hotel, so hopefully we'll be able to whisk you away, but you'll probably have to give an interview at some point. Your friend Beth has been dealing with a lot of the press enquiries, which has been helpful."

I don't look at Theo. "That's good to know," I reply. For the first time, my joy at being rescued tarnishes at the thought that I'm going to have to talk to her. But there's plenty of time for that.

"There was us thinking nobody had even noticed we were gone," Theo says.

"You couldn't have been more wrong." His father smiles. "It's been a good thing. Everyone's been eager to help, which has made it easier for us to get the search and rescue organized."

He pulls the dinghy alongside the plane, where Ben Prince is waiting to help. He extends a hand, clasps mine, and heaves me up out of the dinghy, and I stumble into the cabin.

"Victoria," he says. "Thank God you're okay." He throws his arms around me.

"Hey, Ben." I remember Theo's big brother well. Somewhat stockier and sterner than his gorgeous brother, he was kind and dependable. His hug is extra tight, and I sniffle into his shirt.

"Sit yourself down," he says, moving me behind him to one of the seats. The plane isn't tall enough to stand up in, and I sink gratefully into one of the soft chairs.

He turns back to the entrance and extends a hand to his brother. "Hey, bro."

"Hey, Ben."

"You took your time."

"Felt like I needed a vacation."

Ben laughs and heaves him up into the cabin, and then he throws his arms around him, hugging him awkwardly in the cramped space.

"I thought we'd lost you," Ben whispers, holding him tightly.

"Me, too. I knew you'd find me, though." Theo hugs him back.

"Sit yourself down," Ben instructs. "We'll haul the boat in, and then we'll get you back to civilization."

Nick and Brock climb into the plane, and then the three of them heave the boat into the back before closing the door. Theo slides into the seat beside me, and the two of us buckle ourselves in.

"That word again," I say, adding, "civilization," at his querying look.

He studies my face, concern showing in his blue eyes. "You okay?"

"I feel a bit… odd about going back. A bit panicky. It was so simple, just the two of us. I don't want to have to hold interviews and answer questions."

"You don't have to."

"It's nobody else's business. It was private. That's how it feels, anyway. Am I making any sense?"

"Yes," he says. "Although I doubt anyone else will understand."

"I miss it already." I look out of the window as Ben gets back in the pilot's seat and starts the engine. The island glows in the late sunshine like a jewel, all blues and golds and greens, and a sudden flash of red from a rosella flying through the top of the palms.

I think about the shelter, the Haven, the quiet cave, and feel a deep sense of loss at the thought that I'll never see it again. Yes, it could have been dangerous. It would have been frightening if one of us had been injured. We were only there for ten days, and I have no doubt that if we'd been there much longer it would have ceased to have had any romantic appeal.

But it was our home, and for a brief time we were able to escape the pressures and responsibilities of real life, and concentrate on just being. I'm going to miss that.

Ben turns the plane, and soon we're in the air and the island is receding into the distance. I rest my head on Theo's shoulder, and he kisses the top of my hair. Nick sees him, but at that moment I don't care, and just watch out of the window until the island disappears behind us.

"Whereabouts was the island?" Theo calls out to his father above the roar of the plane.

"Southwest of Fiji," Nick replies. "All the other life rafts were found a long way north of you, which is why it took us a little longer to find you as we began by concentrating on that area. We divided the area up into squares and me, Lucas, Ben, and a couple of other pilots took planes out every day, searching for any signs of habitation. It was only this morning that Kora said she had a strong feeling we were looking in the wrong place. Lucas headed this way on a whim, and he saw your fire this morning. We just had to wait for high tide."

"My dream," Theo says. When we look at him, he explains, "I dreamed I was on the phone to Kora, and I was trying to explain where we were."

"She was convinced she knew," Nick says. He smiles. "You two have always had a connection."

"I think it was Granddad who saved us," Theo tells him. "And Mum. They're both watching over us."

Nick nods, his eyes shining. "I think so too."

Theo's hand finds mine, and we cling together tightly for the rest of the flight.

It takes us a couple of hours to fly back to Suva. Not long at all really, and yet when I look out of the window at the vastness of the Pacific, it's not surprising it took them so long to find us. I doze a little, exhausted from all the excitement, and only rouse when Theo says, "Vic? We're nearly there."

I sit up, my heart instantly pounding. "I don't know if I'm ready to have my photo taken," I joke, putting a hand up to my hair. "I must look a sight."

"You look amazing," he says. "Believe me. I'm an expert."

"He's right," Nick says. "Considering what you've been through, you both look great."

Still, I'm nervous as Ben lands the plane. Surely Nick got it wrong. The only people waiting are going to be our friends and family. Who else could possibly be interested?

But as Ben turns the plane, I can see the crowds gathered on land, the cameras already flashing as we move toward the jetty.

"We'll land at the yacht club," Nick says. "Lucas is the only one here—we didn't think you'd want a family reunion in front of everyone. They'll meet us at the Hibiscus Hotel in the city center. We've got security there keeping the press out."

Theo asks him what's likely to happen over the next few days, but I struggle to concentrate as the plane pulls up next to the jetty. Holy moly, there are so many people! The Fiji police are struggling to hold them back. Many of them are wearing media passes, but there also seem to be a lot of other people waving excitedly at the plane.

"Your fans," Nick calls to me with a smile. "You thought you were famous before? It's a hundred times that now."

The plane stops, and a couple of men rush forward to moor it. Ben switches off the engine, removes his headphones, and turns to face us. "Ready?" he asks.

"The car isn't far," Nick states. "Lucas is waiting to get you into it."

Theo looks at me. "Are you okay?"

I hesitate, half of me wanting to leap out of the window, dive into the sea, and swim back to the island. I can't do this. All those faces, the flashing cameras… I don't enjoy it when I'm freshly washed and with my best clothes on; the last thing I want is to be photographed with messy hair, sunburn, and no makeup.

But there's no way out of it. The media might have hyped it all up, but the truth is that I will have fans out there who have been worried about me. They've supported me all the way, and they deserve to be rewarded now. I can't just ignore them.

"Come on," I tell Theo. "Let's give them what they want."

He grins. "That's the girl I know and love."

It's just a phrase, but it gives me a warm glow as Ben opens the door and jumps down onto the jetty. Nick follows, then turns to help his son down. Theo leaps nimbly onto the wooden pier, laughing as immediately there are a thousand flashes from the cameras. He waves, then turns to smile up at me.

Brock gives me his hand to hold, and I grab onto it as Theo puts his hands on my waist and lifts me down. Another thousand cameras flash, and a huge cheer goes up from the crowd as I land on the jetty. I wave to them, giving them a big smile, half blind from the flashes.

"Bro!" It's Lucas, tall and handsome, enveloping Theo in a bear hug before coming over to me and kissing my cheek. "Hey, Vic. So good to see you."

"Hello, Lucas."

"Let's get you to the car and then to the hotel, eh?"

I nod, and he walks alongside us, guiding us to a waiting limo. A limo! Theo and I stop and turn as we get there and wave goodbye to the crowd, then climb into the car. Ben, Lucas, and Nick also get in, and there waiting for us is Kora, Theo's twin sister, who immediately throws her arms around Theo, sobbing her heart out.

"Hey." He sits on one of the leather seats and pulls her next to him. "Sis, it's okay."

"I didn't think we'd ever find you," she sobs, as I let Ben guide me to a seat opposite.

"Of course you would," Theo soothes, rubbing her back. "I knew when I made that phone call you'd hear me."

She moves back at that, her jaw dropping. "No… you had the same dream?" He nods, and they hug again, as the car smoothly pulls away.

I glance at Ben, who smiles. "You're safe," he says simply. "How do you feel?"

I look around the car. A bottle of champagne is standing in a bucket of ice, and Lucas takes it now and begins to open it. Ice! There's a bowl of fruit, a plate of sandwiches, and a large box of chocolates. I take one and look at it with wonder, then pop it in my mouth. It melts on my tongue, and I give a dreamy sigh.

I have a lot of metaphorical mountains yet to climb, but right now…

"I'm fine," I say to Ben, and smile.

Chapter Twenty

Victoria

It's only five minutes to the hotel. Outside there's another crowd of photographers and onlookers, and we give them a wave as Lucas ushers us into the foyer. For a moment I have the horrific thought that he's going to take us to a huge conference room full of reporters where we're going to be expected to give an interview straightaway. My hair! And I have to brush my teeth before I face any camera.

But he leads us through to a smallish conference room and Nick closes the door behind us. A huge Christmas tree glitters in the corner. A long table groans with food—sandwiches, cakes, little pies, and fresh fruit. My mouth waters to look at them. But there's no time to eat as the room is half full of people who cheer when we go in, and party poppers spray confetti over us as everyone comes up to greet us.

To my left, I see Theo hug Jacob, his other brother, a woman with amazing red hair who must be Heloise, holding a baby who must be Theo's niece Estella, and his grandparents, everyone laughing and crying at the same time. But then I only have eyes for the people in front of me, including my Dad and my stepmother, Gemma, who come rushing up to throw their arms around me. Taken aback, I just stand there, breathing fast, tears pricking my eyes at their obvious relief.

"We thought we'd lost you," my father says in my ear, his hug so fierce I can't breathe.

"I'm okay, Dad."

He lets me go and steps back to look at me. "You're okay? Really?"

"I'm sure I must look awful, but I'm fine."

"You're covered in mozzie bites," Gemma states. "They don't have malaria there, do they?"

"No, luckily."

"I'm sorry," Dad says, and I'm shocked to see tears in his eyes. "For being so caught up with my work. For not having time for you. For… everything."

"It's okay," I reply, my voice husky.

"It's not." He envelops me in a bearhug again. "You're my girl. You remind me so much of your mother, that's all, and it makes me feel so guilty because of what I did to her."

I kiss his cheek. "You didn't do it, Dad. It's something I thought about a lot while I was on the island. It was Mum's choice to take her own life. You didn't do that to her. Theo made me think about how hard it is for people who live with those with depression. I hadn't thought about that before."

"It doesn't excuse what I did."

"No, but it makes it more understandable, and forgivable." I move back from him and look up into his eyes. "I forgive you, Dad. I'm sorry I never said that before."

His chin trembles, and he hugs me again. "I've been so worried. I thought even if you had survived, you'd be starving, or injured, or eaten by wild animals."

I wipe away my tears as he releases me. "The only wild animal on the island happened to be very good at finding bananas." I look across at Theo. To my surprise, he's looking at me, and he laughs at my comment, his eyes full of affection, before turning his attention back to his grandmother.

"They've been so good to us," Gemma says. "The Princes, I mean. They paid for us to fly out here and booked us into the best rooms at the hotel. We haven't wanted for anything."

I don't have time to respond because more people come up to greet me—including the camera crew I work with on Wanderlust Yoga and some of the other staff I employ, many of whom shed tears as they give me hugs and kisses. Everyone wants to know how we survived, what we ate and how we built our shelter. I'm sure they're also all dying to know how my personal relationship with Theo developed, but they're too polite to ask.

There's only one person missing.

"Where's Beth?" I ask Iris, who does research for my visits abroad and organizes places for me to do my yoga program.

"She's had to go to the airport to organize everyone's flights back to New Zealand tomorrow," Iris replies. "She'll be back shortly. She's been rushed off her feet today. Once she heard you might have been found, she went crazy getting everything organized."

"Okay." I don't tell her I'm relieved I had this moment of respite.

"I'm so sorry about Lucy," Iris says, her eyes full of sorrow.

"Yes." I glance around the room, at the balloons, the 'Welcome Home' banner, and everyone's smiling faces. "I feel a bit guilty to be celebrating when so many people died on the flight."

"Don't be silly. It's amazing to have you back. We'll mourn Lucy in our own time," Iris says. "Right now, we're absolutely going to celebrate!"

Ben brings over a drink of cold lemonade on ice and I choose a piece of chocolate cake to eat, which is heavenly while I chat to everyone. It's about fifteen minutes before Nick gets on a chair and calls for quiet.

"I'm sure these two would love to have a shower and a proper meal in their rooms," he says. He smiles at me and Theo. "We'll understand if you are too tired to come back tonight, but you're very welcome to join us once you've refreshed yourself for a proper celebration!"

"I'm happy to come back down," I say, "although I would be grateful for a chance to brush my teeth first!"

Everyone laughs, and Nick grins and jumps down, then beckons for us to follow him. I give my father another hug, then walk with Theo out of the room and across the foyer to the elevators.

Lucas and Ben come with us, and they fend off the couple of reporters who've managed to make their way inside, and ensure Nick, Theo, and I are the only ones who get into the carriage when it opens. The doors slide shut, and the carriage begins to rise.

"Phew!" Theo looks relieved. "I know you said everyone's been watching the news, but I didn't expect quite that reception."

"It'll be even worse when you arrive in New Zealand," Nick says. "The media has gone mad there."

The elevator pings and the doors slide open, and Nick leads us out. We're on the top floor, and as he walks along the corridor, he says, "You both have a suite. Theo, this is yours," he stops by number five, "and Victoria, you're in number six. Your dad and Gemma are in seven, and the rest of us are in the other rooms. I'm in two if you need anything. There's a room service menu in there, just order anything you fancy, or let me know if you want something that's not on there and we'll get it brought in. Now, I have something else for you." He puts his hand in the pocket of his jacket and pulls out two objects and hands one to me. It's a phone—the same make and model as the one I lost. "We've transferred your mobile numbers across so you're all good to go."

I rub my thumb across the screen, feeling the familiar weight in my hand. "Thank you so much."

"Thanks, Dad." Theo stares at the screen for a moment, then looks across at me. "Weird, huh?"

"Just a bit."

Nick hands us our key cards. "Okay, you two." He checks his watch. "It's nearly seven now. Shall I come back up around eight? Is that long enough for you?"

"That'll be perfect, thank you," I say, and Theo nods.

Nick smiles, then gives us both one last hug. "So glad you're back," he says gruffly. Then he strides off down the corridor and disappears into the elevator.

Theo watches him go, and then his gaze comes back to me. We stand there for a moment, studying each other.

"Beth's at the airport organizing the flights," I say eventually.

His smile fades. "Right."

"I need to talk to her, Theo. Before anything else."

"I know."

"But we'll talk soon, right?"

"Yeah. Whenever you're ready."

"Okay. Have a nice shower."

He grins. "You too." He taps the keycard to the door, opens it, and goes inside.

I watch the door swing shut, sigh, and walk down to my own room. I open it with the card and go inside.

It's a huge suite, beautifully decorated in pastel shades of blue and orange and gold. Several green palms bring an extra touch of color. A sofa and chairs face a large TV, and through the door I can see a bed with white covers and turquoise cushions.

I wander across to the windows and look out at the gorgeous view of the Pacific, which is slowly turning to gold in the setting sun. Somewhere out there is the island, with our shelter, the cave, and the Haven, quiet now we've gone.

Swallowing hard, I turn away.

I look down at the phone in my hand as I wander into the bedroom. My thumb hovers over the button to turn it on. Then I toss it onto the bed and go over to open the wardrobe doors. Someone—Beth, I'm guessing—has hung up half a dozen pretty tunics and the kind of long skirts I like wearing, and there are several pairs of sandals on a rack.

I go through into the bathroom, which is huge with white tiles and has both a bath and a shower. I'd love a bath, but I know Nick will be waiting for us at eight o'clock, so for now I turn the shower to hot and set it running.

I'm still carrying the little bag I made. I pull the strap over my head and put it on the shelf. I leave most of the items inside, but I do take out Watson the rabbit and sit him on the hand basin. He looks a little ridiculous next to the shining taps and the classy hand wash, but he makes me smile.

Also on the shelf, someone—Beth again I'm sure—has left a selection of Wanderlust Yoga beauty products, all in my favorite flowery perfume.

I study them, then instead take the hotel's own free coconut shampoo, conditioner, and bodywash. I open the cubicle door and go inside.

Ohhh... it's running hot water, and I stand beneath it for ages, letting it soak my hair and skin, before I pour shampoo onto my hand and massage it in. As I lather it up, it makes me think of when Theo combed it for me, removing all the knots, patient and gentle. At the time, I still harbored resentment toward him because I thought he'd been unfaithful. Now I know he wasn't, I see that act in a completely different light.

My eyes sting, and tears run down my face and mingle with the water from the shower. How much can I cry in one day? But I can't stop, and eventually I dissolve into tears and sob, overcome with relief and a strange kind of sorrow that my adventure is over, and I have to return to real life.

It doesn't last long, and then I scold myself, finish washing, and get out and dry myself. I brush my teeth, taking a long time to ensure they're extra clean. Then I take a look at the makeup Beth has left me. Usually my makeup routine would take half an hour—a touch of foundation and concealer under the eyes, powder over the top, eyeliner and eyeshadow and mascara, lipliner and lipstick... the list is endless.

She's chosen all my favorite brands, and all the right shades. She thinks she knows me so well.

I put a dab of concealer under my eyes and on the couple of mosquito bites on my face and neck. Then I pick up the hairdryer and dry my hair.

Beth has left a large selection of hair slides and scrunchies for me. I ignore them and pick up the plastic clips I found on the island, and pin my hair into a scruffy bun. Then I go back into the bedroom.

I put on one of the long skirts and tunics, ignore the sandals, remaining barefoot, then go back into the other room.

I open the fridge of the minibar, take out a small bottle of Sauvignon, and pour it into a glass. As I swallow the first mouthful, I close my eyes, enjoying the slide of the cool liquid down my throat. On the top of the counter is a basket full of snacks, and I choose a KitKat, smiling as I remember asking Theo if he had one in his pocket on the life raft. That was when he took out his wallet with the condoms.

Still smiling, I open the door and go out onto the balcony.

"What are you smiling at?"

There's a screen that can be pulled up to separate the balcony from the one next door, but it's currently down, and as I turn I see Theo standing on his balcony, looking out at the view.

I hold up the KitKat. "I was thinking about the life raft."

"I never did use the condoms."

I chuckle and go to stand next to him, separated only by a low wall. Breaking off a stick of KitKat, I offer it to him. He smiles and takes it. He's wearing a white polo shirt that makes his skin glow where he's caught the sun, and a pair of navy shorts. He's barefoot like I am. He's had a shower, and he's now clean shaven again. I want to reach up and stroke his jaw and see how smooth it is. But I don't.

"I quite liked the beard," I tell him.

He fingers his chin and gives a rueful smile. "It was a bit itchy." His gaze slides down me. "You look nice."

"Thank you." I have a mouthful of wine.

"Sauvignon?" he says, amused.

"Yeah. Whisky?" He's holding a glass tumbler with an amber liquid.

"Over ice." He swirls it in the glass. "Ice! I thought I'd never see it again."

I laugh, and we lean on the post between us and look out at the view.

"Funny to think of it out there, all alone," I say. "The island, I mean."

"Yeah. Have you still got Watson?"

"He's sitting on the sink. He looks a bit incongruous here."

He laughs.

"Theo, I want to say thank you."

His eyebrows rise. "For what?"

"For looking after me."

"I hardly think you need looking after."

"You know what I mean. I was unwell several times. I don't think I'd have made it on my own."

"Yes, you would. You're stronger than you think."

"I don't know. Maybe. But I know you made it easier. You made it not just bearable, but fun. It was a magical time. And I'm going to miss it."

"Me too." He looks back out to sea. "Have you switched on your phone?"

"No, not yet. I couldn't face it."

"Me either. I know I'm going to have a thousand calls and texts. I might wait till tomorrow."

"I suppose we'll have to return to the real world eventually. But maybe we can wait one more night."

"Yeah."

I have so much I want to say to him. But the words won't come. I need to speak to Beth first. Only when I've done that will I know I'm free to move forward.

He rests his hand on top of the dividing wall, palm up. I slide mine into it. And we stand there like that, watching the sun set, until it's time to go.

Chapter Twenty-One

Victoria

As we take the elevator down to the ground floor, I begin to regret agreeing to rejoin everyone this evening. I'm not in the mood for a big party, and the last thing I want is lots of noise, loud music, and hundreds of people.

I'm relieved to find that rather than holding a huge party in the conference room, Nick has hired out the bar for our friends and family. A table groans with food, and two bartenders serve up the drinks while carols play softly in the background. The fairy lights on the Christmas tree in the corner make the tinsel sparkle. With a glass of Sauvignon in one hand and a plate of delicious snacks in the other, I'm able to mingle and chat to my heart's content.

"How are you doing?" Iris asks me about thirty minutes later. "You look amazing, by the way."

"I'm good, thank you. I feel a lot better for having a couple glasses of wine," I admit.

"I've had several messages from Beth," she reveals. "She's been trying to call you for hours. She's still stuck at the airport."

"I haven't turned my mobile on yet." I don't want to have that conversation over the phone.

"I don't blame you," Iris says cheerfully. "They're more trouble than they're worth sometimes." She doesn't seem to see the irony as she glances at the phone in her hand to make sure she hasn't missed any texts.

"How long will she be?" I ask.

"I think she's finally got the flights sorted, so she should be back any minute. Have you tried these little buns? They're so more-ish."

"I'm good, thank you." I've already had two and could easily eat another two, but the news that Beth will be here shortly makes my stomach flip, and suddenly I can't bear the thought of another mouthful.

I glance across the room, not really surprised to see Theo watching me where he's standing talking to his brothers. Most times this evening when I've looked over, I've found his gaze on me. I lift my glass to him, and he toasts me back before returning his attention to the conversation.

I think of the moment on the island when I first saw the plane. I'd been thinking about making the most of my contraceptive injection, and had been feeling exultant about the fact that I had all that time with Theo alone. When I heard the buzzing, for about thirty seconds I just stood there, fighting with my instinct to turn and go inside the cave and pretend I hadn't heard it. I actually felt disappointed, because I'd finally made the decision that I wanted to be with him, and the plane's arrival was going to change everything. I nearly passed up on the chance to be rescued because I wanted to stay there with him. Will I ever tell him that? Maybe, one day.

First, though, I need to speak to Beth. I finish off my wine, ask the bartender for another, and down half of that. I need the Dutch courage. I'm going to have to speak to her alone somewhere. I wonder whether I'll discover tonight if she really thinks she saw Theo kiss another woman, or if she flat-out lied?

A commotion near the door informs me she's arrived. I glance across the room at Theo. For once, he's not looking at me. He's staring at the door, his expression carefully blank.

I turn and watch her come through. She smiles as our colleagues greet her, although I can see her gaze searching the room, looking for me. She's the same height as me, and a similar build, although she has a tendency to put on weight around her hips and thighs, which she hates. She's as dark as I am blonde. I can see she's had her hair cut since the plane crash. I wonder when she had that done? It must have been while I was missing. That's odd. I don't think I would have done that if it had been the other way around.

Her gaze finally falls on me and she stops walking.

Even from across the room, with several groups of people between us, our eyes meet. And at that moment, I read the truth in them. She lied, and she knows that while Theo and I were marooned together, he's almost certainly convinced me he's innocent.

I turn and walk away in the opposite direction, through the door and out onto the large deck that overlooks the hotel pool.

I sip my wine, looking at the green palms and ferns, the huge colorful flowers, and the still water of the empty pool as I think about the waves on the beach. It takes about thirty seconds before I hear footsteps behind me, and I turn to see Beth walking slowly out onto the deck.

She comes up and stands before me. She's holding a glass of clear liquid.

"Water?" I say, amused in spite of myself.

She sips from it. "I found out yesterday," she says. "I'm pregnant."

I stare at her. It was the last thing I expected her to say. "Congratulations." My voice is flat.

"Thank you." Hers is the same.

We study each other for about thirty seconds. She looks wary, maybe a little resentful. Not contrite. Not guilty.

"Why?" I ask eventually. My fingers tighten on the stem of my glass, and I force myself to relax them.

"Why am I pregnant?"

"Why did you lie to me?"

She looks away for a moment, out to sea. "You were going to throw away everything we'd worked for. Three years at university, all that planning, the organization. You'd have dropped it all for one man."

"You don't know that."

"He was all you ever talked about," she snaps. "You asked his opinion on everything. It was only a matter of time. And then you said you were pregnant, and I knew that was the final nail in the coffin. How were you going to go around the world and run a business with a baby in tow?"

"So what was the plan?" I ask furiously. "Once Theo was out of the picture, were you going to talk me into having an abortion?"

For the first time, she looks uncomfortable. "Of course not. You'd already made that decision, don't you remember? You were worried he'd argue against it. I knew if you stayed together he'd talk you into keeping it. And you were too young to be tied down with children."

"That wasn't your decision to make." My anger and resentment burn with the heat of a thousand suns. "Have you ever thought that maybe the fact I broke up with Theo was a contributory factor to my miscarriage? That the stress and unhappiness made me lose the baby?"

She pales at that. "Vic, come on…"

"I loved him," I whisper. "He was the love of my life, and you made me believe he cheated on me."

"You didn't need much convincing," she says bitterly. "You've always hated men, ever since your dad killed your mum."

Her cruel words hit me like a punch in the stomach. "She chose to take her own life because she suffered from depression and she couldn't deal with his affair. He did something stupid. He didn't kill her."

"You keep telling yourself that if it makes you feel better. The point is, I didn't have to talk you into believing me. You were already primed. You would never have trusted Theo and that would eventually have broken the two of you up. Look what happened with Jack. You couldn't bear to let him out of your sight. You're damaged goods. I did you a fucking favor."

At that moment, all my emotion drains out of me, and all I feel is tired. I don't want to argue anymore.

"We're done," I tell her. "You're fired."

"You can't fire me," she bites back. "I'm a director."

"That's true. Okay, let me put it this way. I quit. The company's yours. I'll be interested to see how you continue to run it without the main star."

She swallows hard, takes a deep breath, then forces a smile on her face. "Vic, come on. We can sort this out. It needn't affect the business. We'll find someone to replace Lucy and we'll hardly have to see each other. It'll be such a shame to throw away everything we've built because of one man."

"A man who's worth a thousand of you. I'm out, Beth. Expect to hear from my lawyer soon. Enjoy your baby. I hope the pregnancy and birth go well."

I finish off my wine, leave the glass on the table, and walk away.

If she follows me, I think I'm going to punch her. But she doesn't. I walk around the hotel, eventually finding another door in via the restaurant. As I enter, people glance up at me and nudge each other, but I ignore them, crossing the room, going out into the foyer, then hitting the button to call the elevator. I stand there with my arms folded as I wait for it to open.

My heart pounds and my eyes sting from a mixture of fury, despair, resentment, and disappointment. I'd so wanted her to continue to insist she'd seen him, as at least I would have been able to persuade myself she hadn't done it on purpose. But this... It makes the last seven years a mockery. All the work we've done, the relationship she and I have had. It's all turned to ashes in my mouth.

The doors slide open, and I walk into the carriage. They're just sliding shut when someone slips in between them, joining me inside. It's Theo.

"Hey," he says. "You okay?"

I press a hand to my mouth and burst into tears.

"Aw, here, come on." He pulls me to him, wraps his arms around me, and holds me tightly as I sob.

Behind my back, he punches the button for our floor, and the elevator begins to rise. Then he strokes my back and kisses my hair while I cry into his shirt.

When the doors finally open, he bends a little, scoops me up into his arms, and carries me down the corridor to my room. He lets me touch my keycard to the door, pushes it open, and goes inside.

It's dark out now, but he doesn't turn on the lights. He walks through to the bedroom, which is lit with silver from the waning moon. Gently, he lowers me onto the bed. I move back so I'm sitting against the pillows and wrap my arms around my knees while he plucks a tissue from the box by the bed and hands it to me.

"Do you want me to call someone for you?" he asks. "Your dad?"

I shake my head and blow my nose. "Don't go," I whisper.

"Want a drink?" he suggests.

When I nod, he smiles and leaves the room. I hear him go into the kitchen, and the sound of wine being poured into two glasses. Then he comes back in. He hands one to me, then goes around to the other side of the bed, climbs on, and sits back against the pillows, crossing his long legs at the ankle.

He holds out his glass. I touch mine to it, and we both take a sip.

"I don't mind if you want to go back downstairs," I whisper. "They must wonder where we've gone."

"I told Dad we were both knackered and needed some rest. He'll make sure everyone's all right. You don't have to worry about anything."

I have another mouthful of the crisp, cold Sauvignon. Theo reaches over to his side of the bed and returns with a bowl of chocolate mints. He offers them to me, and I take one, remove the wrapper, and pop it in my mouth. It's crunchy and sweet, a perfect accompaniment to the wine.

"You okay?" he asks.

"She lied," I reply. "I could see it in her face the moment I looked at her. She wasn't mistaken. She lied because she thought I was going to give up on our plans, and because she thought you'd talk me out of having an abortion." I rest a hand on my tummy as I think about the little life I lost. "She hadn't considered the stress of our breakup might have caused me to miscarry. Hopefully that will haunt her now she's pregnant."

"She's pregnant?"

"Yeah." I look up at him then as guilt sweeps through me. I'm not going to let what happened turn me into a horrible person. "I'm sorry, I didn't mean that. I don't wish her or the baby harm. She's been good to me in many ways through the years, and I hope it all goes well for her. But I told her that I'm quitting Wanderlust."

"You can't quit," he says, amused. "You *are* Wanderlust."

"I know. So it'll be interesting to see what she does with it when I'm gone."

"You shouldn't do that," he says gently. "You should speak to a lawyer and buy her out of the business. It's your company, Vic. You've spent so long building it up. You can't just abandon it now."

I lean my head on the headboard and study his handsome face, his blue eyes that look almost black in the semi-darkness. "It's our company, and although I am proud of what I've achieved, it's turned into something so different from what I first envisaged. All the merchandise, the beauty products, the store… I'm not interested in any of that. I've lost touch with the original reason why we created the company, which was to help other people find peace in such turbulent times. Yoga done properly is a spiritual practice, not a material one, and I lost sight of that."

He opens another mint and offers it to me, then chooses one for himself. "Okay, so what are you going to do?"

I love that he's not arguing with me. He can see how important this is to me, and he understands why I've made this decision.

"I'm going to start again," I tell him. "I'm tired of traveling internationally—it takes too much out of me. I live in the most beautiful country in the world, and I have everything I need right here.

I've been thinking about creating a Haven of my own in New Zealand."

He smiles. "A Haven?"

"A sanctuary. A place where people can come to learn yoga and other spiritual practices like that, to eat healthily, to be creative, and to find peace away from the madness of the world."

"It sounds amazing."

"You planted the seed," I tell him. "With the Haven you created for me. I only got to use it for a few days, but it meant so much to me." My gaze falls to his mouth. "*You* mean so much to me, Theo Prince."

He finishes off his wine, turns, and places his glass on the bedside table. Then he comes back to me, and he slides his hand to cup my cheek, and says, "Can I kiss you?"

"You don't have to ask," I tell him. "I'm yours, and always will be, if you want me."

Chapter Twenty-Two

Theo

"*If* I want you?" I smile. "Silly, silly girl."

Victoria's lips curve up as I press mine to them. She's so soft, this woman, she makes me think of cushions and velvet and comfy duvets and rose petals, all rolled into one.

I feel as if everything that happened seven years ago has been bubbling and popping like lava in my belly since then, and now it's all turned to warm, smooth, sweet caramel.

"I never stopped loving you," I murmur, kissing her face—her eyelids, her nose, her cheeks.

"I don't deserve you." Tears tremble on her lashes. "I'm so sorry I didn't listen to you."

"It's done, Vic. It's so far in the past, I can't even see it anymore. Let's concentrate on how we feel today, and leave the past where it belongs."

"Okay." Her hazel eyes are wide and shining, full of trust. "I love you," she whispers.

"I love you too." I want to show her how much, so I lift her top over her head and tug her skirt off, then peel her panties down her legs and toss them onto the floor. I remove my own clothes, not missing her admiring look as I take off my boxers.

I kiss back to her mouth, then down her neck to her breasts, and pay them some attention for a while, licking and sucking her sensitive skin until they've turned to two hard pebbles in my mouth. I kiss down her abdomen and over her tummy, then shift on the bed and lower myself between her legs. She sighs and stretches her arms over her head, and I part her with my hands and run my tongue right up her core, and she shivers.

"Just relax," I murmur, and I swirl my tongue over her clit and tease it with the tip, encouraged by her long, luxurious sighs.

I take my time, because it's late, it's dark, and nobody's going to be looking for us tonight. I have until the sun comes up to give her pleasure and prove to her I'm here to stay, and having her back in my life is the most important thing in the world.

I know she's changed over the years, but I hope some of the things I remember that she enjoys are still the same. I slide my fingers inside her and stroke her there, then insert the tip of a finger in another, naughtier place, and lick and suck her clit, enjoying her moans and shudders until she clutches a hand in my hair and whispers that she's going to come. Feeling her clench around my fingers is the best Christmas present I could have had, and I hold her tightly until she collapses back on the pillows with a groan.

Slowly, I kiss back up, over her belly and abdomen, her breasts, and her neck, then close my mouth over hers and kiss her for a long, long time.

"Mmm…" she murmurs, looping her arms around my neck as I stroke all the way down to her knees, then back up to her breasts.

"I love your body." I brush my thumb lightly over her nipples. "You haven't changed a bit since we were together."

"I'm sure I have, but thank you anyway." She slides a hand down my back, then brings it around my hip and closes her fingers around my erection. "And you're just as impressive as you always were." She moves her fingers beneath her to gather some of her slippery moisture, then begins to stroke me, her hand gliding over the shaft. I lift my head and look into her eyes, swelling in her hand at her sure, firm touch.

"Yes…" she breathes, her gaze caressing my face. "You're like a loose thread in a sweater, and I'm going to unravel you slowly, Theo Prince, until you come apart at the seams."

I'm starting to lose the ability to form words, so I just kiss her, delving my tongue into her mouth, and brushing my fingers between her legs so I can bring her with me on this erotic journey.

We arouse each other slowly, and we're both more than ready when I finally move on top of her, guide the tip of my erection down into her folds, then slide inside her in one easy thrust. We both sigh, and she wraps her legs around my hips while I lower onto my elbows and kiss her.

I move languorously, lazily, in no hurry to reach the finishing line, and Victoria opens her thighs wide and lets me, her hips rising to meet each thrust. We stay like that for ages, just enjoying being close again, being together. The smell of jasmine floats in through the open doors, warm and exotic, and in the distance I can hear Christmas music and the voices of our friends and families as they join in with an old song. It feels magical, even ethereal, a gift from Santa I hadn't expected.

"Merry Christmas," she whispers, smiling up at me, and I know she must be thinking something similar.

"Merry Christmas." Holding her tightly, I roll onto my back, pulling her on top of me, and she laughs and pushes upright. Now it's her turn to rock her hips and mine to lie with my hands above my head, letting her ride me. I have the added bonus of being able to watch her breasts move with each thrust, and to see the flush spread across her cheeks and throat as her arousal grows, her movements becoming faster and more urgent.

When I can't take it anymore, I tip her onto her back one final time, lift up onto my hands, and begin to move with purpose, plunging down into her soft body. I make sure I'm grinding against her clit too as I move, and it's not long before her breathing turns ragged and I know she's going to come. I'm able to watch her eyes close, feel her clamp around me, just before my own climax hits, and then I can't think about anything else except the blissful pulses as I spill inside her, our bodies locking in hot, sweet joy for what feels like a lifetime.

I open my eyes and look into hers, and know then that I've come home.

*

Later, hungry from all the exertion, we ring room service and order far too much food for two people. We laugh as the waiter brings in a trolley with plates of pizza, fries, sandwiches, cakes, and desserts. But we have a wonderful midnight feast sitting out on the deck overlooking the ocean, eating with our fingers and drinking cold white wine as the warm night breeze blows across us.

Vic is wearing a see-through blue kaftan that reveals more than it hides. I sit in my boxers, enjoying the waft of the Fiji air over my skin.

"So you're definitely going to dissolve Wanderlust?" I ask. I feel sad that for us to be happy, it also means the end of her business.

She nods, leaning back in her chair and propping her feet on the chair in front. "I'm sure you're going to blame yourself for that and imagine it's a negative thing, but I feel lighter of heart than I have for a long time." Her eyes are distant as she looks out at the glimmer of moonlight on the water. "Beth was good to me in many ways. She was always supportive, and she pushed me at times, when it would have been so easy to give up. I know I'll miss her organization and her contacts. But I have enough money in the bank that I can afford to try something different. And now I can take the business in the direction I want. She was always pushing to make it more practical, more materialistic—to concentrate on products and merchandise. But I've never felt that was why I began doing yoga. It's a spiritual thing for me. Not necessarily religious, it's a… a… different thing than that." She blows out a breath and gives me a wry look. "I'm not explaining myself very well."

"Keep going. You're doing just fine."

"Okay, well, for me it's kind of a reaction against the real world, and especially to the Internet. Online, we all tend to create a persona. We post pictures we think others want to see, because all those likes and comments give us a dopamine buzz and make us feel good. But we lose touch with who we really are. Yoga puts us back in contact with that person. Meditation lets us focus on the inner person, the soul, whatever you want to call it. It brings us peace, and I think that's a very valuable thing in today's world."

I smile. "Keep saying things like that, and you're going to do just fine."

Her cheeks flush. "Beth used to mock me a bit when I went all 'airy fairy', as she put it. She thought yoga was all physical, just another way of stretching and toning the body. She didn't like me mentioning the spiritual side of things too much in my videos because she said it turned too many people off. But I think people are looking for that connection. They're searching for more than just a better body shape. They want to feel at peace, and yoga can help with that."

"So you're serious about setting up a Haven?"

"Definitely. As I said, I have quite a bit of money saved, and it should be enough to get it up and running. And it needn't be a place just for yoga. I think we could hold Tai Chi classes, creative writing retreats, watercolor workshops… We could have a restaurant that served healthy food options, and if we pick the location carefully, we could offer nice walks and even a swim in the sea. Maybe a beauty spa with massage, that kind of thing. There could be packages for couples, but I'd also like it to be a safe space for women who come alone. An escape where they can concentrate just on themselves."

"It sounds amazing. I definitely think you're onto something there. And as for the location… I need to speak to Ben first, but I have an idea about that. If you don't mind me interfering."

"Interfere away. I'd be glad of any help."

I'm very happy to give her any aid I can, but I know it's going to be important for this to be her project. She's felt out of control for a long time, and this is her first real attempt to go alone, so she needs to have plenty of freedom to make her own decisions.

"So how do you feel about getting back to the real world?" she asks. "Now we're actually here?"

"The time we had on the island was very precious," I say softly. "And I'll never forget it. But it'll be good to get back to some semblance of normality. We have my grandfather's funeral to get over first."

"Of course, I forgot about that."

"Yeah, it'll be very sad. But then it'll be a matter of looking forward to next year. Dad had already taken over as CEO at Prince's Toys in everything but name, so he'll legally adopt the role, and I'm sure he'll be wanting to put his own spin on things. He's already talking about doing more for charity. Grandad used to donate toys at Christmas, but Dad's going to contact Brock's brother, Charlie King. The Kings own a business called the Three Wise Men. They make medical equipment for children with respiratory problems. He wants to coordinate with Charlie about us making regular contributions toward their research programs. And they also run the We Three Kings Foundation, I don't know if you've heard of it?"

"Oh yes. They grant wishes for sick children, don't they?"

"That's the one. Dad and Ben are thinking about running programs where they transport sick and underprivileged children to the South Pole for the day and give them free toys. He's got all sorts of plans."

"And how do you fit into it all?" she asks, smiling.

"Oh, I'll do whatever's needed. I might fly up to the Bay of Islands and meet with the Kings face-to-face with Dad. Or I can hold the fort in Wellington while they get it sorted. I don't mind. I don't have any major aspirations. I love what I do and I like helping people. I'm happy enough. Especially now." I hold out my hand, and she slips hers into it.

"It was nice to meet Heloise," she says, rubbing her thumb across my knuckles. "She's obviously head over heels for Ben, and vice versa."

"Yeah, it's great to see that after what he's been through."

"And how's Kora doing? Is she going to be part of the work with the Kings?"

I sigh, my brow furrowing for the first time. "Kora is a bit… lost. She had a bad breakup not that long ago, and since then she's been quiet and withdrawn. We're both thirty now, and while that's not old by any means, I think her biological clock is ticking, and she's starting to be concerned she's not found Mr. Right. She threw herself into setting up the antique exhibition at the South Pole, but since then she's been a bit aimless. Dad's been talking about sending her to the UK."

"Oh, why?"

"It's where Arthur Prince had the first family toy store, in Regent Street. He's the one who sold the doll to Queen Victoria."

"The one Ben recently got back?"

"Yeah. Of course the store is now huge with outlets all over England. We're in contact regularly online with the Princes who run it, but sometimes it's nice to meet in person. So she might go and make a few connections, have a look around their stores, and see what they know. She'd like to visit some of the museums in London. It would be good for her to do something different. It might breathe a bit of life back into her."

Vic squeezes my hand, and I know she can see how worried I am about my twin. "It's so funny how you both had the same dream. You obviously have a special connection."

"Most people would say it was a coincidence, but yeah, I think so. It's not as special as the connection I have with you, though." I lift her fingers to my lips and kiss them, and she smiles.

"We should go to bed I suppose," she says somewhat regretfully. "It's going to be a busy day."

"This time tomorrow we'll be home."

"You know we're going to have to do some kind of TV interview," she says.

"Probably, yeah. Hopefully we'll be able to put it off for a few days." I link my fingers with hers. "What do you want to do when we get back? About me and you, I mean?"

I know what I want, but I'm not sure how she wants to proceed. It's such an unusual situation. Do we just take up where we left off? The way she's been acting toward me suggests she's interested in making a go of it, but maybe she wants some time to herself while she reorganizes her business and her life.

"I've been thinking about that," she says. "And I thought... how do you feel about starting again? About going on a few dates, getting to know one another again? Taking it slow, and seeing where it leads us?" She gives me a hesitant smile.

"So... I should wait a few weeks before I dig the ring out of my sock drawer?"

A beautiful smile spreads across her face. "You kept it?"

"I did. I'd propose now, but I suppose it makes sense to wait a couple of weeks for decency's sake."

I get to my feet, pull her up, and lead her into the bedroom. We get into bed, and she stretches on top of me. Her blonde hair falls around my face like a curtain.

"Do you think we'll ever go back to the island?" she whispers.

"Would you like to?"

"I don't know. Maybe. Or maybe we should leave it where it is—as a magical memory."

I take her face in my hands. "I'm just crazy about you. I hope you know that."

Her eyes shine in the moonlight. "I'm crazy about you too, Theo. I never stopped loving you."

And I kiss her, because that's the best Christmas present a guy could ever have.

Chapter Twenty-Three

Transcript of the Rise and Shine TV program, broadcast on January 21st, featuring an interview with Theo Prince, Marketing Director of Prince's Toys, and Victoria Sullivan, star of the Wanderlust Yoga video series. Interviewers: Janine Martin and Frank Evans.

Janine: Good morning New Zealand and welcome to Rise and Shine! Thank you so much for joining us.

Frank: Yes, good morning everyone. We have a packed program for you today, and later we'll be discovering several ways to keep up with those New Year's Resolutions we all make to be fitter and healthier, including some fantastic summer recipes with Louise Brimacombe, and a simple exercise routine suitable for all fitness levels with ex-All Blacks star Greg Foster.

Janine: That's right, and we also have a tour of some of the best beaches in New Zealand, so stay tuned for that.

Frank: But first, we have something very special for you. The week before Christmas, I think everyone in the world had their eyes glued to the TV and the Internet following the news that a flight from Fiji to New Zealand had been struck by lightning and had crashed into the Pacific Ocean, causing the deaths of many of its passengers.

Janine: Yes, it was a tragic accident, and our hearts go out to all the families of those still missing. We are very sorry for your loss.

Frank: Amazingly, thirty-seven passengers found their way into life rafts, and within a couple of days they were all found on neighboring islands and rescued.

Janine: And then the news came out that one of the survivors had seen another life raft bearing two other passengers—the Marketing Director of Prince's Toys, Theo Prince, and the famous yoga presenter Victoria Sullivan from Wanderlust Yoga, who we've had on this show many times.

Frank: Just a few days later, the news broke that Theo and Victoria had once dated seven years ago. Something about this captured the imagination of the public, and soon it was all everyone was talking about, wasn't it?

Janine: Absolutely, we were all caught up in the romantic notion, weren't we, of Theo and Victoria being stranded together on a desert island. Everyone was glued to the news, and then on Christmas Day the wonderful announcement came that they'd been discovered on a tiny island miles from Fiji.

Frank: It really was amazing. I think the whole of New Zealand tuned into us on Christmas afternoon to see them arrive on the seaplane at Suva.

Janine: I cried buckets when they got off the plane! It was a fantastic moment. Well, a few weeks have passed, during which the Internet has been rife with speculation about what happened to them. They've been spotted a couple of times out and about in Wellington, but they haven't given any interviews about their experience… until now.

Frank: Yes, we have a wonderful treat for you all today, because Theo and Victoria are here with us to tell us all about their adventures! Welcome, you two!

Theo: Thank you!

Victoria: Thanks, guys, it's great to be here.

Janine: We really appreciate you taking the time to be here today. I have to add that apparently our viewing figures today are the highest we've ever had with people tuning in all over the world to watch this!

Victoria: Goodness!

Theo: I feel like Brad Pitt.

Frank: The two of you have certainly shot to stardom over this. I have to ask, did you have any idea when you were on the island that so many people would be watching you when you got back?

Victoria: Absolutely not. We said at one point that we had the feeling we'd get back and everyone would be like, oh, have you been away?

Janine: Well, it certainly isn't like that! Everyone is fascinated to hear what happened to the two of you after you got into that life raft.

Theo: We'd both like to start by saying our hearts go out to everyone who lost someone that day, and I hope nobody thinks we're trying to capitalize on the accident by giving this interview.

Victoria: Yes, I think you're putting a phone number and a website across the bottom of the screen right now—we've set up a fund for the families of those who are missing, and please contact them to make a donation.

Janine: Absolutely, and that's a wonderful thing you've done there. And of course none of us thinks you're capitalizing on the accident. Such a great loss of life is terrible, but that doesn't mean we shouldn't celebrate the lives of those who survived.

Frank: That's so true. And you have such a story to tell!

Theo: It was and it wasn't. In many ways it was very simple. We made our way to land and waited for someone to rescue us.

Janine: We all know there was more to it than that. Tell us about how you felt when you found yourselves alone in that raft.

Victoria: It was incredibly scary. The weather was awful, and we had no food and no way to signal for help. It was all we could do to cling on for dear life.

Theo: What we didn't know was that we were the last out of the plane, and the storm pushed us in the opposite direction to all the other rafts. We drifted for miles to the south-west, whereas most of them went north-west. So for the first week or so, the planes were looking for us in entirely the wrong area.

Victoria: We drifted for two whole days. I was terrified, and I know if it wasn't for Theo, I'd probably be dead right now.

Janine: Aw...

Theo: Don't listen to her. She's tougher than she makes out.

Victoria: Maybe, but he kept talking to me, and he was insistent all along that we'd eventually be rescued. Oddly, even though it was a frightening experience, it was also magical too. I remember seeing a couple of whales, with their flukes rising out of the sea.

Theo: They were orcas.

Frank: Wow, that must have been something.

Victoria: Yeah, and also lying awake at night in the bottom of the raft and looking up at the stars. There was no light pollution, and it was amazing. Terrifying, but amazing.

Theo: It was. But yes, also terrifying. We had no food, and we could only drink when it rained. We were severely dehydrated by the time we found land.

Janine: That must have been some moment.

Victoria: It was. We bumped into some rocks just off the coast of a tiny islet. We paddled to shore and collapsed on the beach.

Theo: It was so hot when the sun came out. We'd tried to hide beneath my shirt, but we were both already quite burned.

Janine: So you were shirtless by this point?

Frank: Steady…

Janine: I'm just asking the questions that our viewers will want us to ask.

Frank: Let's try and remain focused. So what was the first thing you did?

Theo: Victoria was quite unwell at this point, severely dehydrated. I scouted the beach and discovered some coconut trees. I managed to open a couple on the rocks so we were able to eat and drink for the first time.

Victoria: I remember feeling very low and panicky. I kept thinking about what would happen if we were sick or injured. We take so much for granted in our everyday lives, and suddenly all that had been stripped away. We had nothing. We were going to have to do everything ourselves.

Janine: That must have been so daunting.

Victoria: Well, Theo's grandfather taught him in the Scouts, and his training came in very useful.

Theo: Yeah, a lot of what he taught me when I was a kid came back to me. We explored the island and discovered that luckily we'd landed in the best area. So we set to making a shelter. Vic wove us lots of mats out of palm fronds…

Victoria: And Theo went fishing. Of course, I'm vegetarian, so that was tough…

Theo: She didn't complain, though. We got by until we found the taros and bananas later on.

Victoria: And the chickens!

Theo: Oh yes! Wild chickens. The eggs were a great find.

Frank: How on earth did the chickens get there?

Theo: We have one theory. Later on, we discovered a cave higher up, and we found evidence that someone had been living there back in the nineteen-fifties. His name was Henry Cavendish. We've done some research since we've been back, and we discovered that his wife, Mary, and his eight-year-old son, James, both died in a car crash in 1956. Henry couldn't get over their deaths, and in 1958 he got on a boat and left New Zealand, heading for Fiji. We don't know whether he crashed on the island or whether he was looking for somewhere to stay, but I think he went there on purpose.

Victoria: Yes, we think he took the chickens with him, and he also had some books and other bits and pieces that were really useful for us, like a pocketknife.

Janine: Oh, that's so sad. What happened to him?

Theo: We don't know. I suspect he died, although we never found a body, but the bush was really thick and we didn't cover every inch, so it's not surprising.

Frank: That's such a poignant story. Did it change how you felt about being stranded yourselves?

Victoria: That's a really good question. Yes, it did a bit. I felt very thankful that I wasn't alone. It would have been a completely different experience if that had been the case.

Janine: And of course you two knew each other before, didn't you?

Frank: Yes… and here's the real story everyone's interested in.

THE CASTAWAY BILLIONAIRE

Theo: Ah.

Victoria: We knew this was coming.

Janine: Well you have to admit, it is quite a story. Because you didn't know you'd both be on the plane, did you?

Victoria: No, not at all.

Frank: We understand that you'd dated previously. We don't want to pry… well, we do, but we're trying to be polite…

Theo: Yeah, we dated for about six months. We'd rather not say too much about why we broke up.

Janine: But you both still had feelings for each other? I can see by the way you're looking at one another I've hit the nail on the head there.

Theo: I think you can safely say that, yes.

Frank: So here were two people who once dated, who'd been split apart by circumstances they had no control over, and who'd been brought together by Fate, in a way that forced them to be alone and confront their past.

Victoria: That's a very romantic way of putting it. But it's true!

Janine: So did you find time to talk about your relationship?

Theo: I think that was inevitable really. You can keep busy during the day, and then crash out at night, while the weather's good. But it was the rainy season, and we were hit by one of the biggest thunderstorms I'd ever seen. We took shelter in the cave, and that was it really—in circumstances like that, there's little to do except talk.

Victoria: So yes, we did talk about our past, and we cleared a lot of things up. It was a very poignant evening for both of us.

Theo: You realize your face is beetroot-red right now?

Victoria: I'm aware of that, thank you.

Frank: All right, we really don't want to embarrass you. Let's summarize by saying you made up, right?

Theo: We did. And time heals many wounds. Emotions are always raw in the moment, but we'd had time to think over what had happened, and we both felt able to move on at last.

Janine: And the next morning you saw the plane?

Victoria: Yes, I couldn't believe it. It was so weird.

Janine: I understand you brought Watson the rabbit home with you—the toy you found on the beach.

Victoria: Yes, here he is! I'll always keep him to remind me of my time on the island.

Frank: So, all in all you were there for ten days.

Theo: Yeah, it's not that long in the scheme of things, but at the time when we didn't know if we'd be rescued, it felt like forever.

Frank: Did the experience change you? Not just in your relationship with each other, but in yourselves?

Theo: It made me appreciate my family even more. They never gave up on me, and we'll both always be thankful for that.

Victoria: Definitely. And yes, it changed me, too. I hadn't been happy for a while. I loved Wanderlust Yoga and I was thrilled how far it had come, but I was ready for something new.

Janine: Yes, so tell us about that. You're talking about opening a health resort, right?

Victoria: Yes, that's right. Well, it turns out that the land next to where Theo's brother lives, in the Abel Tasman National Park, is up for sale. I put in an offer, and we found out this morning it's been accepted.

Frank: Oh, congratulations!

Victoria: It already has a large house built there, but we're going to add to it and develop it. It'll probably open toward the end of the year. It's going to be called Kingfisher Haven, and it'll be a retreat, a place you can go to do yoga and creative pursuits, to eat healthily, and just to find peace.

Janine: Well, we hope you'll come back on Rise and Shine and tell us all about it when it's up and running.

Victoria: Definitely, thank you.

Frank: So… we have to ask… what about the two of you? You said you'd cleared up what happened in your pasts. It's obvious to us, watching you sitting here, holding hands, that you're both very fond of one another. And you know how all our viewers have followed your journey. Would it be too forward of us to ask whether the two of you are back together again?

Theo: Yes. We are. And we're getting married!

Victoria: Theo!

Theo: What?

Victoria: I thought we weren't going to tell everyone yet.

Theo: Eh. I'm the happiest man in the world. I wanted to share!

Janine: Oh, I don't believe it, you're really engaged?

Victoria: We are. He asked me to marry him two days ago.

Frank: That was quick. I like your style.

Theo: Well I still had the ring from seven years ago.

Frank: You were going to ask her back then?

Theo: Yeah. Fate intervened. And then when we got back from the island, we decided we'd try to date normally for a while and see how things developed.

Victoria: That lasted about... forty-eight hours, wasn't it?

Theo: Maybe forty-nine.

Victoria: Then I moved in with him.

Janine: Oh, how wonderful. Let's see the ring, then! Oh wow, that's what I call an engagement ring. It's beautiful.

Victoria: Thank you, I love it.

Theo: Yeah, it was quick, but what our adventures did teach us is that life is short, and you really do have to go for it if you see an opportunity. *Carpe diem* and all that. I love Victoria, always have, always will. Why wait?

Frank: Absolutely. I think that's amazing news, and I know the whole world is joining in with us when we say congratulations, and we hope you'll be tremendously happy together.

Janine: I think I'm going to cry.

Victoria: Me too!

Frank: Me three!

Janine: So there you go, everyone, a fairytale ending! Hopefully we'll have Theo and Victoria back on in the future to let us know how the wedding went, and to see how Kingfisher Haven is progressing.

Frank: Definitely. And before we cut to Louise with details of her new healthy recipes, maybe you two could grant the world what everyone's been waiting to see… a kiss?

Theo: If you insist.

Janine: Oh… and look at that. Isn't that just the best ending you've ever seen? Thank you for watching. I'm sure you'll join me in wishing the two of them—and Watson—a very happily-ever-after.

Newsletter

If you'd like to be informed when my next book is available, you can sign up for my mailing list on my website, http://www.serenitywoodsromance.com

SERENITY WOODS

About the Author

USA Today bestselling author Serenity Woods writes sexy contemporary romances, most of which are set in the sub-tropical Northland of New Zealand, where she lives with her wonderful husband.

Website: http://www.serenitywoodsromance.com
Facebook: http://www.facebook.com/serenitywoodsromance

Printed in Great Britain
by Amazon